A Viking's Shadow

A VIKING'S SHADOW

A CHIEF INSPECTOR SHADOW MYSTERY

H L Marsay

TULE
PUBLISHING

DEDICATION

To Jason, Harry and Charlie.
Thank you for your love, support and encouragement,
but mainly for throwing the best book launch parties ever.

Acknowledgements

My thanks to the magnificent team at Tule: Jane Porter, Meghan Farrell, Cyndi Parent and Nikki Babri.

I was so lucky to work with three amazing editors: Sinclair Sawhney, Helena Newton and Beth Attwood. Many thanks for all your suggestions and your patience.

Thanks also to Patrick Knowles for another wonderful book cover and to Lee Hyat for coordinating the design.

CHAPTER ONE

Across 10 (6 letters)
This Norseman may be the Romans' number six monarch

IN YORK, IT was six o'clock on a Friday evening in late September. The sun was already beginning to set, and a cool wind was blowing through the city. Detective Chief Inspector John Shadow cursed under his breath as he edged slowly along Parliament Street. He was pressed up against a metal barricade put in place to hold back the crowds. To his right visitors and locals alike pushed forward. To his left marched the Great Heathen Army. They were shouting and cheering loudly as they held axes and burning torches aloft.

A six-foot-tall Viking strode by with a long, red, plaited beard, flowing green cloak and brandishing a gleaming broadsword. His impressively convincing appearance was spoilt only by the mobile phone tucked neatly into his woven leather belt. Shadow always noticed these small details about people, even if he did endeavour to avoid their company.

York held its annual Viking Festival every year in September, to coincide with the ancient Heathen feast of Haustblot. The idea was to celebrate the city's Norse heritage. After all, it was the Vikings who called the city Jorvik, that eventually became the modern-day name of York.

Usually Shadow avoided the city centre like the plague when the festival was on; somehow this year it had slipped his mind. From the moment he'd stepped out of the station, he'd been caught up in the crowds. Now he was trapped. A middle-aged man of average height with slightly greying dark hair, in a suit and wax jacket, his unremarkable appearance now made him stand out. His every step was blocked by either camera-toting tourists in fake beards and plaits or excitable small children with wooden swords and horned helmets.

Shadow's empty stomach grumbled in complaint. At this rate, he would never make it to Francesco's. He adored Italian food and each night ate in one of the city's many excellent restaurants. It should only have been a five-minute walk over to La Scuola Femminile on Petergate, but tonight it was going him to take much longer.

Finally, the Norse warriors and their followers spilled out into St Sampson's Square. Shadow strained his neck. He thought he could see a path through. However, just as he was about to make his escape, he found his way blocked by a familiar red-haired figure holding a Dictaphone.

"Have you got a quote for the *Herald* readers regarding this year's festival, Chief Inspector?" asked Kevin MacNab, a journalist from the city's local paper and one of Shadow's least favourite people.

"Not one you could print," growled Shadow in response as he pushed his way past.

Making a swift escape was going to be harder than he'd hoped. The whole of St Sampson's Square had been turned into a Viking village with tents dedicated to various aspects of the life of the average Norseman. There was a weaving demonstration in one and a blacksmith was forging a sword in another. In the next tent Shadow found Edward Bennington, one of the city's leading experts on Vikings. Edward owned a bookshop on Fossgate. This evening he was retelling the history of King Ragnar and his warring sons to an enraptured audience.

"The vengeful Anglo-Saxons threw brave King Ragnar into a pit of snakes to kill him; and his sons – Ivar, Ubba and Sigurd – swore vengeance…"

Edward's voice was thin and reedy, but Shadow had to admire the effort he had put into his costume, complete with an eye patch and a raven perched on his shoulder. In the audience, Shadow spotted his colleague Sergeant George Hedley. His little grandson was sitting on his lap and looked completely enthralled. George caught his eye and Shadow raised his hand in silent greeting.

As Shadow continued, he passed a lady with long grey hair selling sourdough bread that smelt tantalisingly good. Martin Plunkett, a local solicitor, was wearing a fake beard and seemed to be having a disagreement with the tall Viking warrior who was manning the beer tent. Shadow shook his head. It was clear the whole city had gone totally Viking mad. He took a few more steps before he felt a tap on his shoulder and heard a cheerful voice in his ear.

"I didn't think this was your sort of thing, Chief!"

Shadow turned and scowled at the grinning face of Sergeant Jimmy Chang, his deputy.

"Where have you been all day?" he asked impatiently.

"I've been really busy investigating the protection racket, Chief."

Recently, there had been a spate of smashed shop windows and Jimmy was convinced there was more to it than mere coincidence. Shadow groaned loudly.

"I've told you before this is North Yorkshire, not Naples! We don't have protection rackets."

"But, Chief," protested Jimmy, "ten businesses with broken windows in less than a month! There's something dodgy going on."

"There will be a simple explanation. It'll be down to drunk students, out of control after a night in the pub, or an attempted burglary by an inept thief."

"There's never any witnesses or video surveillance footage. Nothing is ever stolen and it's small independent businesses, like kebab shops or off-licences that are always targeted." Jimmy was determined not to be put off, but Shadow shook his head, not convinced.

"Exactly! Just the sort of places where a few young lads might end up after a heavy night drinking."

"Well, the one last night was different. It was the toy shop on Lord Mayor's Walk and this time something was taken."

"Really? What?" Shadow asked in surprise.

Jimmy looked down and shuffled his feet before he reluctantly replied. "It was a blue fluffy rabbit."

Shadow barked out a laugh. "Oh well, that's it then," he scoffed. "The mafia have definitely infiltrated York. It may be over twenty-five years since I worked for the Met and had to deal with organised crime, but I distinctly remember the sole motivation of hardened gangsters was the acquisition of soft toys."

Before they could argue any further, the detectives were interrupted by two drinking horns being thrust between them. The bearer was Sophie Newton, one of the pathologists they worked with.

"Evening, gentlemen! Here, have this. I thought it might cheer you both up. Neither of you look like you're exactly channelling the spirit of the Vikings!"

Sophie, on the other hand, had clearly fully embraced the festivities. She was wearing her hair in long blonde plaits beneath what seemed to be the obligatory horned helmet.

Both policemen thanked her, and Shadow took a large, grateful swig, but instead of the hoped-for drink of refreshing beer, his mouth was filled with an unfamiliar sweet, spicy liquid. He grimaced as he swallowed it down.

"Crikey, Sophie! What is it?" he asked, trying hard not to

cough.

"Mead," explained Sophie, "fermented honey with cinnamon. It's what the Vikings used to drink and is made to a traditional recipe, apparently. They called it, 'The Drink of the Gods,' and it's meant to turn anyone who partook into a poet or a scholar. Don't you like it, Chief?"

"It must be an acquired taste." Shadow frowned as he sniffed the drink suspiciously. "Or maybe that's why the Vikings invaded England in the first place. They were simply looking for a decent drink." Then realising he sounded ungrateful: "Sorry, Sophie, it was a nice thought."

"No problem." Sophie shrugged. She didn't look offended. He reasoned she was probably used to his occasional tendency to sound grumpy by now.

"I think it's all right," said Jimmy as he took another swig. "Cheers, Sophie. The plaits suit you, by the way."

"Thanks, Jimmy!" She beamed.

"But you do know the real Vikings didn't actually have horns on their helmets," added Shadow.

Sophie rolled her eyes at Jimmy before turning back to Shadow. "Don't you start, Chief! Mr Bennington has already given me a ten-minute lecture on the subject. He's quite the expert! Anyway, shouldn't you be at Catania's or Little Sicily or somewhere?"

Shadow's routine of eating at various Italian restaurants on different nights of the week was also well known to those he worked with.

"Yes, I should," he complained, indignantly. "I was planning on going to Francesco's place, but all the streets have been blocked off to create this chaos!"

The three of them continued slowly around the Viking village, passing tents selling leather belts and carved wooden trinkets. They came to a halt in front of a tent where a pretty, blonde young woman in a rather low-cut tunic was offering to tell your fortune using ancient Viking rune stones.

"All right, sweetheart, do you want to cast the runes and see what the gods have in store for you, darling?" she asked, leaning forward and giving Jimmy a flirtatious smile. Her strong cockney accent among all the northern voices made her stand out even more than her revealing dress.

With his usual good-natured grin, Jimmy agreed and handed over his money. He shook the small leather pouch she handed him and then emptied the smooth square stones, with their carved symbols, out on to the table. The young woman made a big show of waving her hands around and studying the runes. Shadow suspected that, like all fortune tellers, she was better at reading people than the runes.

"The stones say you are ambitious, and you have a bright future," she announced. "There has been both happiness and sadness in your past. I see a mysterious blonde woman in the stones and conflict with a dark-haired man. Beware of the letter E. Oh, and you'll have very good luck in love. I'm not surprised – a handsome lad like you," she finished with a

Jimmy blushed slightly as he thanked her.

"Who knew lipstick was so readily available back then," murmured Sophie quietly into her horn of mead, only loud enough for Shadow to hear.

"What about you, sweetheart? Do you want to know what the gods have in store for you?"

The fortune teller had now turned her attention to Shadow.

"Thank you, but no." He smiled politely. He had no interest in what the future might hold unless it was to show him a quick route through this crowd.

Suddenly, the mass of Vikings began to cheer loudly. Everyone turned to look as a large man of about fifty years old, with long dark hair, streaked with grey, strode on to the platform. He placed his hands on his hips and the breeze caught his red velvet cloak, so it flowed out behind him. It was an impressive sight. The rune girl gave an excited squeal and blew him a kiss. Shadow thought he looked vaguely familiar. In a deep booming voice, the man on the platform addressed the gathered army.

"I, King Ragnar, welcome you all to our great city of Jorvik." He paused while the cheers died down. "My Viking friends, together we shall celebrate our noble heritage, honour our mighty ancestors, and feast like the gods. I therefore declare this year's Festival of the Vikings officially open!" He dramatically drew his gleaming sword and jumped down from the platform. The Great Heathen Army gave another deafening roar and banged their swords against their shields as they started to march after their leader. Shadow watched as King Ragnar exchanged a passionate kiss with the rune girl and pressed a small parcel into her hand, before leading his troops on.

"Where are they all off to now?" he asked, hoping it was away from Petergate, so he might finally be able to make it to his table at Francesco's.

"King Ragnar's leading his troops back to the Viking encampment," explained Sophie.

"Which is where?"

"St George's Field car park."

"Well, they're lucky we've had such a dry start to September, otherwise it would be flooded. It often is this time of year. It doesn't seem like the most sensible location to choose."

"I suppose they needed to be close to the river for the longboat race. It's been advertised as one of the highlights of the festival. Twelve traditional Viking longboats to race by torchlight from Skeldergate Bridge to Millennium Bridge and back."

"For crying out loud!" Shadow exclaimed.

He pressed his horn of mead back into Sophie's hand and hurriedly began to push his way through the crowd.

"Was it something I said?" Sophie called out after him.

Shadow didn't bother to reply, but he could hear Jimmy

simply say, "*Florence.*"

FLORENCE WAS THE name of the narrow boat where Shadow lived. She was moored on the River Ouse, a little way down from Skeldergate Bridge. The thought of a dozen boats crewed by amateurs carrying naked flames, heading towards her at speed, filled him with horror.

Hoping to outmanoeuvre the Vikings, who were marching towards Coppergate, he turned on to Market Street, then hurried on along Spurriergate and Tower Street. He reached Skeldergate Bridge just in time. Crowds of onlookers were beginning to gather, and, in the distance, he could hear the roar of the approaching army.

Down on the bank of the river the twelve longboats were moored, the shields lining their sides decorated with brightly coloured geometric designs or images of dragons and eagles. On the other side of the river he could almost make out the shape of *Florence.* Her red roof and red and black sides were darkly silhouetted against the sky, but her name painted in gold and the flowers surrounding it glinted in the moonlight.

Shadow crossed the bridge and dashed down the towpath, startling the geese, who honked loudly at him. He reached *Florence* as the Vikings arrived at the bridge. Swiftly, he untied the mooring ropes, jumped aboard, pushed off from the bank with his foot and started the engine. A few moments later, he was travelling downriver towards Fulford.

As *Florence* chugged quietly along, the shouting and cheering from the longboat crews grew fainter. When she slipped beneath Millennium Bridge, the halfway point of the race, Shadow looked over his shoulder. He could see the glow from the torches. They were obviously on the river now and heading his way. To be safe he steered *Florence* on for another quarter of a mile and moored her next to Fulford Ings.

He was confident the longboats would not come as far as the nature reserve, although he was amazed the city council had given permission for the event to go ahead at all. In his experience, they were usually obsessed by health and safety. Any dead tree in the public parks was promptly chopped down before it could fall on a passer-by, and they had even been known to tarmac over cobbled streets for fear someone may trip and hurt themselves. Yet they had allowed hordes of people holding burning torches and assorted weaponry to congregate by the river in the darkness; it was strange to say the least.

When *Florence* was safely secured to the large iron mooring ring on the riverbank, Shadow could finally step inside the boat and relax. He went straight through to the bedroom and took off his jacket and tie, glancing over at the photo of Luisa as he did so.

He wondered what she would have made of the Viking Festival. No doubt she would have thrown herself into enjoying it. She was from southern Italy and far more sociable than him, not that that was difficult. He remembered how she had once cajoled him into going to the Notting Hill Carnival when they lived in London.

Luisa had loved the Caribbean music and brightly coloured costumes. He could picture her now, tossing her long dark hair as she joined in the samba dancing, while he self-consciously shuffled along next to her. With a sad shake of his head, Shadow closed the bedroom door behind him. It was over twenty-five years since he'd lost her in a car accident, but he still missed her like it was yesterday.

As well as the bedroom and bathroom, *Florence* had a compact galley and comfortable living area. Shadow lit the small wood burner opposite the large, squashy sofa, then went in search of something to eat. The contents of his fridge could, at best, be described as sparse. There was, however, some leftover Sorrento ham and a loaf in the bread bin that was just on the right side of stale. He sighed. It wasn't the pollo farcito he'd been hoping for, but it would have to do.

His thoughts drifted back to Luisa. She had been an amazing cook. She could open a cupboard or fridge and, no matter what she found there, would create the most amazing dishes. He'd watch her simply throw ingredients into a pan, then ask her how she knew what she was doing without a recipe. She laughed at him, as she often did and said simply, *instinct*. It didn't matter how many Italian restaurants he visited, nobody cooked like Luisa.

Shadow poured himself a large glass of Chianti, put on his favourite Frank Sinatra CD, and settled down on to the sofa. With his sandwich on one side and his unfinished *Yorkshire Post* crossword on the other, he could finally begin to unwind. He took a sip of wine and swilled it around his mouth then swallowed it with a satisfied sigh. Finally, the lingering, sickly sweet taste of the mead was banished. He decided to relax and leave it a couple of hours before heading back, by then the madness should have died down.

A little while later, the crossword was complete, Frank had finished singing "How About You" for the second time, and the fire had died away to a few glowing embers. Shadow pulled his old battered wax jacket back on and ventured outside to the deck. He strained his ears and eyes, but all seemed quiet.

He cast off from the riverbank, turned *Florence* around and headed back to the city. The moon was shining brightly in the clear sky and his breath formed clouds in the cool night air as *Florence* quietly glided back under Millennium Bridge. Shadow tutted to himself as he spotted floating debris from the race. An extinguished torch, abandoned shield, even a false beard floated by.

He approached Skeldergate Bridge with some trepidation. Although the boat race might be over, he was sure the Viking festivities would continue long into the night. However, as the bridge came into view, it wasn't the warm glow of burning torches that greeted him, but bright blue flashing lights.

A tall thin figure in a black leather jacket was jogging down the towpath in his direction. Shadow steered towards the bank and threw him the mooring rope.

"I take it there's a problem, Sergeant?"

"We've got a body, Chief," replied Jimmy as he tied a knot in the rope, tightly securing *Florence*'s position.

Shadow ducked inside to put his jacket and tie back on. He couldn't say he felt especially surprised at Jimmy's news. The more he'd thought about it, the more the whole staging of tonight's event seemed to him utter folly.

"Drowned or burnt?" he enquired as he stepped off the boat and on to the towpath.

"Neither, Chief. A stabbing. Someone has stuck a thirty-inch sword right through King Ragnar."

CHAPTER TWO

Down 6 (5 letters)
Ulfberht's sharp words are etched here

KING RAGNAR WAS in reality Alfred Campbell. He was one of York's wealthiest and most well-known businessmen. His photograph was often featured in the local press, which was why he had seemed so familiar to Shadow. About twenty-five years ago, he had discovered a hoard of Viking treasure on farmland he owned, on the outskirts of Fulford.

His share was worth millions and he became rich overnight, selling most of the treasure to museums and collectors. He had, however, kept a few choice pieces and using his new fortune set up various Viking-themed ventures in the city. Along with the annual festival, there was the Daneholm museum with a shop that catered to tourists and school parties. He had also opened Asgard's bar and even a night club, called Valhalla, both named after the Viking idea of heaven.

As the two policemen made their way back over the bridge, Jimmy filled Shadow in on what had happened. After the longboat race had finished, King Ragnar, or Alfred, was due to present the victorious crew with a trophy, but he was nowhere to be seen. Edward Bennington, the secretary of the festival, had gone in search of him and discovered his body in "King Ragnar's Palace" and called the emergency services immediately.

"Is Sophie with the body?" asked Shadow.

Jimmy shook his head. "No, she's not on duty tonight. We'd just left at the end of the race when I got the call and came straight back."

"I see." Shadow nodded, quietly noting the way Jimmy had said "we'd just left", but more concerned that this meant he would have to deal with Donaldson, the other, far less amenable pathologist.

Despite the late hour, there was still a large crowd of Vikings and tourists gathered outside the encampment, trying to see what was going on. Shadow stepped across the cordon. He nodded his thanks to the uniformed officers, who were doing their best to keep control, helped by a few burly security guards in fluorescent jackets.

The encampment in St George's Field car park was more elaborate than the one in St Sampson's Square. Instead of tents, several low wooden structures with roofs almost sloping to the ground had been erected. The largest of these was decorated with animal skulls and had the words *King Ragnar's Palace* painted above the door in Nordic-style letters. A young constable held the door open for Shadow and Jimmy as they approached.

"Thank you, Constable. Don't let anyone through without my say-so," ordered Shadow.

"Certainly not, sir. It's Tom by the way, sir," replied the young man eagerly.

"Thank you, Tom," said Shadow as he stepped across the threshold.

INSIDE THE PALACE, painted shields and more animal skulls and horns covered the walls. Long wooden tables with benches ran along each side and there was a smouldering fire in the centre of the room with the smoke drifting up to a hole in the roof. At the far end were two carved wooden throne-style chairs with a heavy black curtain hanging behind.

"The body's through here, Chief," said Jimmy as he pushed aside the curtain.

Shadow stepped through into a smaller anteroom. Another fire surrounded by stones was burning on the floor of the room. There was a wooden bed covered in fur throws pushed against the wall. There was also a fur rug on the floor beneath the body. In the centre of the room were two wooden chairs and a table.

Jimmy began busily using his phone to take photos from various angles. Shadow took in the details of the scene while trying very hard not to look directly at the wound and the copious amount of blood on the floor. Despite a career in the police that spanned over thirty years, Shadow was still incredibly squeamish.

The dead man's hands were resting on the hilt of the sword. There was a length of black silky material covering his eyes and tied around the back of his head. On the table was an open bottle of expensive French red wine and two full glasses. *No mead in a horn for King Ragnar*, thought Shadow. By the way he'd fallen, it looked like Alfred was sitting on the chair with his back to the curtain before the sword had struck him and he'd slumped down on to the floor.

"What are you thinking, Chief?" asked Jimmy, switching on his electronic notebook, ready to begin taking notes.

"I'm thinking that for such a brutal death, it's a remarkably peaceful crime scene. No signs of a struggle. The glasses haven't been knocked over; there's not even a single drop of wine spilt."

"Wow, you're right! Do you think he did it to himself? It does look like he's holding on to the sword handle."

"Hilt," Shadow corrected him automatically. "Suicide is a possibility, I suppose," he conceded, without much conviction.

"Or maybe someone entered, threatened him with a gun so he didn't move or try and fight back, then stuck the sword in him?" Jimmy continued.

"Then why not use the gun to kill him?" replied Shadow,

humouring his sergeant, although privately he was sceptical of the idea. In his experience, guns were rarely a feature of crimes in the city. They were certainly not as readily available as Jimmy might imagine.

"Too loud?" offered Jimmy.

"Perhaps," mused Shadow, but he was distracted by something else. There was a heavy scent of perfume in the air. It was strong enough not to be masked by the wood smoke from the fire. He knew he'd smelt it before, but he couldn't remember where or when.

"What about the blindfold? That's a bit weird isn't it, Chief?"

Before Shadow could answer there was a commotion outside and Donaldson came storming through the black curtain, followed by Tom, the harassed-looking young constable.

"I'm sorry, sir, I couldn't stop him," said Tom. Shadow waved away his apology and Tom scuttled back through the curtain.

"What sort of an operation are you running here, Shadow?" demanded Donaldson. "That young lackey tried to stop me coming in. Aren't they taught to recognise those people whose presence is vital to an investigation?"

Shadow raised an eyebrow. Donaldson was one step away from uttering the most pompous question of all: "Don't you know who I am?"

"Well, you're not exactly dressed for the occasion. What

have you come as?" asked Shadow.

Donaldson was stood before them in what appeared to be a Scottish fancy dress costume. He was wearing a tartan kilt, complete with sporran, white frilly shirt, short black jacket and white knee socks. Jimmy failed to stifle a snigger. Donaldson glared at the two detectives and replied haughtily.

"I'll have you know this is formal Highland dress. I happen to be the president of York's Saltire Society. We were enjoying our annual ball at the Merchant Adventurers' Hall before your ill-timed interruption."

He strode over and looked down at the body on the floor.

"Poor old Alfred, eh? Straight through the liver by the look of things. Not a bad chap, I suppose, if a little rough around the edges."

"You knew him?" asked Shadow.

"I played golf with him once. He and Gillian made up a four with myself and my good lady wife."

Shadow rolled his eyes. The pathologist never missed an opportunity to let the chief inspector know that he was on first-name terms with his boss: the chief constable of North Yorkshire. Donaldson was now kneeling next to the body and peering at the wound.

"I assume even you two don't need me to tell you the cause of death." He smirked sarcastically as he opened the neck of Alfred's shirt, exposing the dead man's chest and shoulders including a tattoo of a strange pattern of lines and symbols he couldn't make out. Jimmy bent down to take a photo of it.

"Do you think it could have been suicide?" he asked.

Donaldson frowned and elbowed the sergeant out of the way. "I appreciate your faith in my diagnostic skills, Sergeant Chang, but even I can't ascertain the state of mind of a corpse."

"But the wound could have been self-inflicted?" persisted Shadow.

Donaldson threw a dismissive glance towards the chief inspector before examining the fingers around the hilt of the sword. "It is a possibility, but looking at the position of his hands, I'm not convinced. I'll know more when I have him on the slab."

"And time of death?"

"Within the last hour," replied Donaldson as he stood up. He had clearly decided his work there was done.

A thought suddenly occurred to Shadow. "He wasn't a member of the Saltire Society, too, was he?" he asked, gesturing to the body.

An expression of disdain crossed Donaldson's face. "Hardly! He wasn't really our type and you know what they say: the only good Campbell is a dead Campbell."

With that the pathologist turned and strode back out of the room without bothering to wish the detectives good-night.

"That was a bit harsh even for him," complained Jimmy,

then mimicked Donaldson's voice: "*The only good Campbell is a dead Campbell.*"

"Oh, I think it was only clan pride talking," replied Shadow, then seeing Jimmy's blank expression: "The Glen Coe Massacre?"

Jimmy shook his head and Shadow sighed. For someone who had grown up in York, a city virtually dripping in history, his sergeant sometimes displayed a shocking lack of historical knowledge.

"Campbell soldiers were given shelter by the MacDonald clan in Glen Coe, but instead of being grateful, the next morning the soldiers woke up and killed thirty members of the clan in cold blood. With a name like Donaldson, our charming doctor clearly feels an affinity with the MacDonalds."

"Whoa!" exclaimed Jimmy, looking horrified. "When did all this happen?"

"The late 1600s, I think. There's been bad blood between the two clans ever since."

"Talk about holding a grudge," murmured Jimmy, shaking his head incredulously. "I didn't even know Donaldson was Scottish."

"He's not. He was born in Kent. Then again, I doubt many of those marching in the Great Heathen Army had a drop of Scandinavian blood in them either."

"That's why I never really got History, Chief. Leave the past in the past – that's what I say."

Shadow didn't bother to respond; he was distracted by something he'd seen at the edge of the fire. Fishing out his glasses from his pocket, he knelt down to take a closer look. It looked like a smouldering wallet. Cautiously, using his pen, he nudged it out of the flames and into the ashes to cool. As he was about to stand up, he noticed there was a collection of tiny smashed pieces of glass or plastic next to one of the large stones surrounding the fire and yet nothing in the room seemed to be broken.

"When forensics get here, ask them to take a look at all this," he said, pointing to the charred wallet and the fragments. "Where are they anyway?"

The forensics team were both young and quite new to the city. Privately Shadow referred to them as Laurel and Hardy, as one was tall and skinny and the other short and fat. They tended to talk only in scientific jargon, so he usually left Jimmy to liaise with them.

"Ollie phoned to say they are on their way, Chief."

"Who?" asked Shadow, a little startled.

"Ollie, the short one with dark hair."

"Please tell the other one isn't called Stan."

Jimmy looked puzzled and shook his head.

"No, he's Ben. They were both here, so they had to leave and go to fetch all their equipment. Now they're stuck in traffic."

Shadow shook his head. Ben and Ollie might know all the latest scientific procedures, but Shadow sometimes found them lacking when it came the basic skills, like timekeeping.

There was a small cough outside and Tom put his head through the curtain. "Sorry to interrupt, Chief Inspector Shadow, Sergeant Chang, but Mr Bennington, the gentleman who discovered the body, is waiting outside. Would you like to speak with him tonight or shall I let him go home, sir?"

"No, ask him to come through by all means, thank you, Constable – I mean Tom."

A moment later, a rather nervous-looking Edward Bennington stepped cautiously through the curtain. He was a small, slightly built man with grey thinning hair that he had pulled back into a short ponytail. He had removed his eye patch and the bird on his shoulder had disappeared. His tunic, trousers and cloak were all in earthy green and brown tones. Shadow thought that no doubt they were more authentic, but they lacked the glamour of Alfred's costume. He stepped forward and shook Edward's hand.

"Thank you for waiting, Mr Bennington. I understand you've already met Sergeant Chang."

"Oh yes, I must say Sergeant Chang got here very quickly after I called." Edward smiled and gave Jimmy a small wave.

"And what time was that?" asked Shadow.

"It must have been a little after nine. I can't be more exact I'm afraid, Chief Inspector, as I wasn't wearing my watch. I like to be as true to the Vikings as possible. I even forgo my spectacles. Now that would have been an anachronism!" He gave a little chuckle. "But back to your question. The race was due to finish at nine. We all thought it a bit odd Alfred wasn't there. Normally, he would have been standing on the bridge, cheering the boats on.

"As secretary of the festival, it was my job to find him, so the prizes could be awarded. I don't suppose they shall be now. What a waste," he lamented, but Shadow couldn't be sure if he was referring to Alfred or the prize-giving ceremony. He thought Edward didn't seem particularly perturbed by discovering a dead body, but his eyes did keep flicking over to where the corpse lay. Shadow motioned to Jimmy to cover Alfred. Reluctantly, Jimmy began to unzip his jacket. Edward held up his hand to stop him.

"Before you do, may I?" He gestured towards the body. "I doubt I'll get another opportunity. I expect you'll have to take everything away," he explained with a sad look on his face.

"Yes of course, Mr Bennington, but please don't touch him," agreed Shadow, thinking perhaps Edward was close to Alfred after all. Grief could affect people in strange ways. Edward knelt next to the body and the two detectives respectfully took a few steps back and lowered their heads. Shadow wondered if he would say a prayer or perhaps wanted to wish Alfred a last goodbye.

"It's incredible, such exquisite detail," they heard him murmur. Jimmy looked up at Shadow and raised an eyebrow. Edward was peering intently at the sword. He didn't seem to mind that at least half of it had been left buried in someone who, Shadow assumed, was a close acquaintance, if not a friend.

"Is it a special sword?" he enquired.

Edward remained transfixed. "It's an Ulfberht sword, Chief Inspector. Of course, the original is in the Daneholm museum. Nobody can use that. This is only a replica, but a stunning example nonetheless. Alfred had it specially commissioned for the festival.

"Ulfberht was a master swordsmith of the Viking age. Before him, swords were made of soft iron bars welded together with strips of steel, shaped into a blade then adding a steel edge. Ulfberht was the first to make a sword out of good quality steel, and he improved the design so it was more tapered and better balanced. In those times, it was as significant as inventing the combustion engine. You see these etched markings? They honour Ulfberht and his skill."

"Is it valuable?" asked Jimmy and Edward smiled.

"It would be impossible to put a price on something so beautiful," he sighed.

Shadow cynically raised an eyebrow. He suspected that wasn't true.

"Can I ask why he called himself King Ragnar? Why not King Alfred?" enquired Jimmy. Edward looked at him as if he were mad.

"The leader of the Great Heathen Army could hardly use

the name Alfred, Sergeant! King Alfred was the Anglo-Saxon leader who inflicted such a heavy defeat to the Vikings at the Battle of Edington. No, Alfred Campbell might be able to buy himself whatever he pleased, but he couldn't change the name he was born with. During the festival, he chose to call himself King Ragnar. Alfred was always fond of role play, thought he was quite the thespian, and after all Ragnar Lothbrok, King of Sweden and Denmark, was the father of Ivar the Boneless, who founded our great city."

Shadow could see Jimmy was about to ask another question, caught his eye and shook his head at him. This was no time for an impromptu history lesson.

"Did you see anyone else here when you discovered the body?" Shadow asked, trying to steer the conversation back to the investigation, unsure if he was wasting his time. He doubted any judge would thank him for calling Edward as a witness.

Edward stood up and gave his head a little shake, as if awaking from a dream. "No, no not a soul, Chief Inspector. Well, I don't think there is anything else I can tell you, so I shall wish you goodnight, gentlemen." He gave another little wave and disappeared back through the curtain. Jimmy and Shadow could hear him quietly whistling as he walked away.

Shadow shook his head and yawned loudly. "Well, I think that's enough excitement for me for one night. I'm going home. Can I leave you to wait for forensics to come and arrange to have the body moved?"

"No problem, Chief," replied Jimmy, still sounding cheerful despite having to work so late.

"And make sure uniform get statements from everyone. Somebody must have seen something."

"Will do," Jimmy called after him.

Shadow left Ragnar's Palace and walked through the empty encampment to the police cordon, where a sizeable crowd was still gathered, straining their necks to get a look at what was happening. No doubt it wouldn't be long before MacNab and the rest of the press arrived too.

As he walked back over Skeldergate Bridge, various questions were beginning to vie for attention in his head. Where was the blonde-haired cockney fortune teller who had kissed Alfred so passionately? Who was the second glass of wine for if not her? And if Edward was so authentic in his costume that he wouldn't even wear glasses and a watch, whose phone had he used to call the police?

CHAPTER THREE

Down 1 (9 letters)
It's strange to initially get the low-down on feeling choked

DESPITE NOT GETTING to bed until after midnight, Shadow was up, showered, dressed, and making his way back into the city centre by eight o'clock the next morning. After having to make do with supper at home the previous evening, he was determined not to miss out on his full English breakfast at Bettys. York's oldest and most famous tearooms was already busy when he arrived. He took a seat at his usual corner table and unfolded this morning's copy of the *Yorkshire Post* crossword. Julie, his petite dark-haired regular waitress, approached him with a welcoming smile.

"I'll have my usual, please, Julie," he said, not bothering to look at the menu or the specials chalked on the black-board.

"Are you sure about that, John?" she queried.

Shadow looked up at her in surprise. He had been coming here for years and his morning order never varied. Julie nodded towards the window overlooking St Helen's Square.

Jimmy had his face pressed up against it. He waved as soon as he caught Shadow's eye and motioned for him to come outside.

"For crying out loud," groaned Shadow under his breath, then turned back to Julie. "I know you don't normally do takeaways, Julie," he began.

She smiled softly and patted him reassuringly on the arm. "I'm sure the kitchen will make an exception for you, John. I'll go and have a word."

A few moments later, Shadow stepped outside with a bacon muffin wrapped in a paper napkin in one hand and a disposable cup full of tea in the other. It wasn't the full English he had been hoping for, but it was certainly better than nothing. Jimmy was standing on the pavement, fiddling with his phone. He looked up when he saw Shadow.

"Sorry to interrupt your breakfast, Chief, but we've had a call to say another body has been found."

"Really? Where?"

"Down in St Sampson's Square, at last night's other Viking encampment. A security guard found her first thing. It's the girl who told my fortune with the rune stones."

"Well, that explains why she wasn't in Ragnar's Palace," murmured Shadow as he took a sip of tea then a bite of muffin.

The two men turned and made their way down Parliament Street, retracing Shadow's footsteps from the night before. It had rained heavily during the night and the grey paving stones were still glossy and wet. Council workmen in bright orange jackets were busy dismantling the barricades from the previous evening's march of the Great Heathen Army and it felt strangely subdued after all the crowds and commotion.

As the pavement was still narrower than usual, Jimmy walked a couple of paces ahead. He looked like he was doing a strange sort of dance, as he swayed from side to side, his long legs sidestepping the many puddles that lay in his path.

"New trainers," Shadow said, more as an observation than an enquiry. He shuddered to think what his sergeant spent on his footwear.

Jimmy nodded. "I wouldn't have worn them if I'd known it was going to be this wet," he complained.

"Yes, who could possibly have envisaged it would rain during autumn in North Yorkshire?" retorted Shadow as he took another bite of bacon muffin.

They arrived in St Sampson's Square and came to a halt at the fortune teller's tent. The outside was already draped with bright yellow police tape, while two uniformed officers patrolled up and down.

"You go in and check what we've got," Shadow said between mouthfuls. He was enjoying his breakfast too much to have it ruined by a beheading or some other gruesome wound. Jimmy ducked into the tent. Shadow took his last bite, wiped his fingers, and screwed the napkin into a ball and stuffed it into his pocket.

"It's okay, Chief. She's only been strangled," Jimmy's voice shouted out loud and clear from inside the tent. An old lady pulling a shopping trolley along behind her looked startled and stopped to stare. Shadow smiled weakly before also ducking into the tent. He was relieved to see that Sophie was the pathologist on duty this morning.

"Morning, Chief," she said cheerfully. "Nothing too grisly for you this morning." She lifted the plastic sheet to reveal the body of the blonde woman who had told Jimmy's fortune with the rune stones. Her face, with its closed eyes, looked strangely serene, but there was a plaited fabric rope wound tight around her neck.

"Strangled by her own belt, by the look of it, but there isn't the discolouration I would expect. However, there is some bruising to the back of head I want to look at properly. I'll be able to give you a more accurate time of death too, but my best estimate right now is between twelve and fourteen hours," explained Sophie. Shadow nodded. That meant she was killed at roughly the same time as Alfred.

With her latex-gloved finger Sophie pointed to the victim's hands that were folded together neatly across her chest.

"If you look closely, Chief, you'll see each of her fingernails are still perfectly manicured. I don't think she tried fighting off whoever did this to her."

"And she was found like this?" asked Shadow. The way she was laid out resembled the marble effigies covering the ancient tombs in the Minster.

Sophie nodded. "Yes, it's strange, isn't it?" she agreed. "It almost looks like she's sleeping."

Shadow was still staring at the victim's hands. On her left wrist was a gold band. He rummaged in his pocket for his glasses so he could see it more clearly. The metal was twisted and at either end was an intricately carved cat's head studded with sparkling stones.

"Have you taken a picture of this?" he asked Jimmy as he pointed to the bangle.

"Not a close-up, Chief. Why? Is it important?"

"Well, she wasn't wearing it last night when we spoke to her."

Jimmy bent down with his phone, while Shadow turned his attention to a waxy substance on the floor, with a line scratched through the middle.

"And what's this down here?" he asked.

"Forensics have taken a sample, but I think it's probably from the candles that were burning in here," replied Sophie, pointing to a wrought-iron candelabra holding three candle stubs and covered in long thin drips of solidified creamy-white wax.

"And the scratch?"

Sophie gently lifted the hem of the victim's long skirt. Beneath, she was wearing a pair of very high, shiny black stilettos.

"They found a trace of wax on one of the heels too, Chief."

"Well, they really are an anachronism! Mr Bennington certainly wouldn't approve," chuntered Shadow. He turned back to Jimmy, who was busy tapping on his notebook.

"Have we made an identification?"

Before Jimmy could reply, Sophie pointed to a leopard-print purse on the floor.

"Forensics found that on a shelf under the table, but you're okay to touch it. They said no fingerprints except the victim's," she said.

Jimmy picked up the purse, unzipped it, and gave a low whistle.

"There must be over two hundred quid in cash in here, maybe we should take up fortune telling, Chief." He rummaged further. "And according to her bank card, her name is Chloe Campbell."

"A relative of Alfred's?" asked Shadow.

"I don't know, but it can't be a coincidence can it, Chief?"

"I doubt it," sighed Shadow. He was remembering the kiss Alfred and Chloe had shared last night and the package he had observed Alfred handing over.

"Oh well, at least Donaldson will be happy – another dead Campbell," joked Jimmy.

Sophie gave a snort of laughter. "Yes, he takes his self-appointed role as York's MacDonald clan chief very seriously, doesn't he?"

"Do you know about the whole Glen Coe thing?" asked

Jimmy.

"Oh yes, and it's not just Donaldson. My mum's family is from round there. Once we went for lunch at this pub and the sign above the door read: 'Dogs allowed, no hawkers, no Campbells'."

"Really?" Jimmy grinned. "I didn't know you had relatives up in Scotland."

"Oh yes, my granny grew up on a croft in the Highlands. She spoke Gaelic before she spoke English. I remember her trying to teach me; it's a really beautiful language."

"Can you still speak it?"

Sophie shook her head. "No, she died when I was ten and sadly the only word I can remember is *Seanmhair*."

"What does that mean?"

"Grandma," she said with a smile.

Shadow frowned. His deputy and the doctor seemed to be getting sidetracked and there was something else bothering him.

"Sophie, can I ask you a personal question?" he asked.

Sophie gave him a slightly wary look but nodded her head. "Sure, go ahead," she replied.

"Do you carry a handbag?"

"Yes, but only a small one. I keep it in one of the outer zip compartments," she gestured towards her large black medical bag.

"And what do you have in there?"

"Purse, keys, phone, hairbrush, some clips, a nail file, a

lip balm, not much."

Shadow looked at Sophie's make-up-free face, then his eyes returned to Chloe with her manicured nails and face covered in perfectly applied cosmetics.

"Then where is her handbag?" he asked. "I understand her keeping the purse close to her while she was telling fortunes, but surely she would have her make-up and hairbrush in a bag somewhere in here."

"Well, if she did, it's not here now. We'd have found it," said Sophie with a shrug.

"But if the murderer stole the handbag, why not take the purse full of cash?" joined in Jimmy, as he quickly made a record in his notebook.

"Exactly!" agreed Sophie.

"Well, I don't think we're going to find out any more here," said Shadow with a nod. "Thanks for your help, Sophie. Let us know about the bump on her head when you can."

The two detectives stepped out of the tent. Fortunately, it was still fairly quiet in the square.

"We need to speak to the next of kin and find out what the connection is between Chloe and Alfred," said Shadow. "And get on to forensics. I know they have been busy here this morning, but I still need to know what, if anything, they found at last night's scene. I'll be back in a minute."

"Sure, Chief, see you soon," replied Jimmy, already dialling one of the numbers in his phone.

Before he did anything else, Shadow needed to buy some indigestion tablets. His grumbling stomach was complaining loudly about him eating his breakfast on the move. He spotted a chemist's shop on the other side of the square and hurried over. After completing his purchase, he stepped back out into Parliament Street, feeling much more comfortable with two tablets dissolving in his mouth.

"Well, fancy seeing you here!" said a very loud and familiar voice. Shadow turned to see Maggie Jackson heading towards him. She was an old school friend and owned the dry cleaner's and laundry where Shadow often took his washing. He swallowed the tablets quickly. Maggie was gripping on to a lead attached to a huge black Great Dane. It was unclear who was walking whom.

"Morning, Maggie." He smiled. "I didn't know you had a dog?"

"I don't!" she exclaimed. "This brute belongs to my son, but he's swanned off on holiday to Spain leaving muggins here in charge. Oh, do stop pulling, Harald!"

The Great Dane was panting and wagging his tail furiously as he strained on the lead. Shadow guessed that if Harald was to stand on his hind legs, he would be at least a foot taller than Maggie.

"Are you two off for a walk?" he asked.

"Yes, I'm taking him down to the river, which will hopefully tire him out. I thought I'd do you a favour at the same time and drop these off on your boat while I'm down there."

She raised her free arm to show a plastic bag containing two of Shadow's freshly laundered shirts.

"That's very kind of you…" he began, but Maggie waved away his thanks as she twisted the lead more tightly round her wrist.

"It's nothing and I didn't think you'd have time to collect them with these two murders to investigate."

Shadow looked at her incredulously. "How do you know about them already?"

Maggie gave him a sympathetic smile. "You can't keep secrets in this little city, John, especially not when Alf Campbell is involved. Of course, I could have told you it would all end in tears."

"What would?"

"Alf and Chloe! I mean, a more than thirty-year age gap is one thing, but to go off with your daughter-in-law?"

Maggie chattered away so quickly Shadow had to really concentrate on what she was saying to keep up.

"Let me get this straight, Chloe was married to Alfred's son?"

"Yes, Dan, such a nice good-looking lad, but I'm not sure if you could really call it a marriage when it happened up in Gretna. I heard they were looking to get an annulment, not a divorce. Anyway, it was a bit of a whirlwind romance, but then she met Alfred and between you and me, I think Chloe thought why wait for Dan to inherit when she could be enjoying all that lovely money now. Of course, it's

Annabel I feel really sorry for."

"Annabel?"

"Dan's mum – Alf's ex."

At that moment Harald shook his head, sending a long string of drool into the air that landed back on his head.

"Yuck!" exclaimed Maggie. "I had better get going and pray he doesn't find any geese on the river to chase or he'll drag me in, and you'll have another body on your hands."

Shadow watched as Harald dragged her away. He felt as though he'd just been hit by a very short and noisy hurricane. He popped two more tablets into his mouth. His indigestion was worse than ever now.

Jimmy was still waiting, phone in hand, outside Chloe's tent where Shadow had left him.

"Everything okay, Chief?" he asked, cheerfully.

Shadow scowled. "Not really – I'd like to know why the city's biggest gossip is better informed than my officers?"

Jimmy waited with an expectant look on his face, but as was often the case, Shadow didn't elaborate any further. He was lost in his thoughts. Jimmy tapped open his notebook and cleared his throat.

"Well, I spoke to forensics. They said the only blood spilt last night was Alfred's. When it came to fingerprints…"

"Let me guess? None, but Alfred's," interrupted Shadow.

"Actually, no, the opposite – too many and mostly smudged. It seems people were in and out of that room a lot. Alfred must have been a sociable guy. They managed to lift a few fingerprints off the blindfold, but they were only Alfred's and none at all on the sword handle."

"Hilt," Shadow corrected him.

"Sorry, Chief, hilt," Jimmy apologised quickly. Having his meals interrupted always put Shadow in a bad mood and this morning was no exception.

"What about that broken glass by the fire?"

"It was something called Gorilla Glass. They use it to make the screens of mobile phones."

"Did they find Alfred's phone?"

"No and there was no sign of his keys either. The wallet in the fire was definitely his. The credit cards were still in, but had mostly melted – and no cash."

"I see," said Shadow as he thought for a second. "That reminds me, find out whose phone Edward called from."

"Will do, Chief," replied Jimmy as he made a note for himself.

"Okay, what else?"

Jimmy scrolled back a couple of pages. "Finding out exactly who is the next of kin wasn't that straightforward, but I spoke to uniform, who have already sent someone to break the news. Alfred has an ex-wife…"

"Annabel," Shadow interrupted, taking Jimmy by surprise.

"Er yes, Chief, and Chloe had a husband, although I believe they are estranged. His name is…"

"Dan," supplied Shadow again. If Jimmy wondered how

his boss had become so well informed during his brief trip to the chemist, he knew better than to ask.

"Have you got an address, Sergeant?" asked Shadow.

"Yes, Chief, Annabel lives over in Fulford and I believe Dan lives there too."

"Right then, let's go." Shadow turned on his heel and began briskly walking towards the river. Jimmy looked up at the sky. Fulford was over two miles away and rain clouds were already beginning to gather.

"Oh, Chief," he pleaded, "can't we take a car?"

Shadow paused and looked back at him with a frown on his face. "It's not that far. You're just worried about messing up those fancy new trainers."

"It'll take forever, and it looks like rain." As Jimmy spoke a few drops of rain began to fall from the sky.

Shadow relented with a shrug. "Oh, all right then, but don't go above thirty and no using the siren."

ON THE LONG list of things Shadow disliked, being a passenger in a car – particularly when Jimmy was driving that car – was fairly near the top. Although no longer drove himself, he had a habit of slamming his foot down on the floor and constantly shouting out "Brake!" whenever he thought they were getting too close to the car in front.

On the way to Fulford, Shadow finally filled Jimmy in

on what Maggie had told him about the relationship between Alfred and Chloe.

Jimmy shook his head in disbelief. "What sort of a father would do that to his own son?"

"A bad one!" muttered Shadow, digging his nails into the sides of the chair as Jimmy swerved to avoid a pigeon.

Neither Shadow nor Jimmy had children of their own and they had both lost their own fathers when they were young, so had little experience of a father-son relationship. It wasn't something the two of them ever discussed, but Shadow felt certain that dating your son's ex-wife would surely be difficult to forgive.

"You said Dan and Chloe got married in Gretna?" queried Jimmy.

"Yes." Shadow nodded. "Gretna Green is one of the first towns you come to when you cross the border into Scotland. Their marriage laws were historically more relaxed than those here in England, so it became notorious as a place for couples who wanted to elope. Traditionally they joined hands over an anvil, as the blacksmith's was the first building they arrived at. I believe it's still popular when you want to get married in a hurry."

"I wonder if that's why Dan and Chloe went there?"

"Maybe. By the way," said Shadow, "you said a security guard found Chloe's body."

"Yes, uniform spoke to him. They said he'd only been on duty for ten minutes when he found her."

"Which company had the contract to provide the security for the festival?"

"A company called AAB Security, Chief. They must be new. I've never heard of them."

"Neither have I," agreed Shadow.

They continued driving south, out of the city for a couple of miles. Through the drizzling rain they passed the cemetery and Imphal Barracks. Fulford had once been a village in its own right, but over the centuries it had been swallowed up to become another suburb of York.

THE CAMPBELL FAMILY home was at Battlefield Farm, on the main road. The farmhouse itself was over three hundred years old and the village had grown up around it. It was a long, low stone building with a thatched roof. It looked strange standing on the side of a busy road with a small parade of modern shops opposite. Any farmland that must have once belonged to it had obviously been sold off and was now covered in a new development of neat, identical red-brick houses.

The two detectives stepped out of the car and approached the house. Although Shadow knew two uniformed PCs had already been and broken the news of the two deaths to the family, he still felt a sense of trepidation as he knocked on the front door. Despite his years of experience, it was often impossible to know how the bereaved would react. Sometimes they were angry, sometimes sad, and sometimes simply disbelieving.

His knock on the door was greeted immediately by a cacophony of loud barking from inside the house. A few seconds later, a woman's voice could be heard hushing the dogs and telling them to be quiet.

"Hold on! I'm coming!" she called out.

The front door was opened by a petite woman whose long grey hair was held back from either side of her face by two tortoiseshell combs. It was the same woman Shadow had seen selling bread the night before. She gave the two detectives a bright smile but was clearly struggling to hold back her canine companions.

"Good morning, I'm Detective Chief Inspector Shadow and this is Sergeant Chang."

The woman wiped a floured hand on her blue-striped apron and offered it through the gap.

"Annabel Campbell – that nice policewoman left not long ago but she said you might call round. Please come in but do try not to let the dogs escape."

Shadow and Jimmy exchanged a quick glance before edging their way carefully through the narrow opening into the house and quickly shutting the door behind them. They then made their way slowly through the hallway, whilst attempting to fend off the enthusiastic welcome of two terriers and a whippet.

"Don't worry – they don't bite," Annabel reassured them. "It's just their way of saying 'hello'."

The two detectives followed her into the large farmhouse kitchen. It was a bright, sunny room. There was a quarry-tiled floor, pine units lining the walls and a deep white Belfast sink beneath the window overlooking the large garden. Shadow noticed items of Viking-style clothing on the washing line, flapping in the breeze.

In the centre of the room was a huge scrubbed pine table covered with bowls, flour, spoons, and a rolling pin. By the look of things, they had interrupted a busy pie-making session. Shadow sniffed the air appreciatively; the smell reminded him of his own grandmother's kitchen. She had been a farmer's wife and an excellent cook.

A large blue Aga took up most of one wall. On top of it was a pile of neatly folded laundry and on top of that was a snoozing tabby cat, curled up. A black Labrador was also fast asleep and snoring loudly on a large tartan cushion laid in front of the Aga.

"This one's not much of a guard dog," commented Jimmy, bending down to stroke the sleeping dog.

Annabel smiled indulgently. "Oh, poor old Winston! He's as deaf as a post I'm afraid, but he always manages to wake up when it's dinner time."

Suddenly a small alarm clock, perched on the table, began to ring.

"I won't be a minute, gentlemen," Annabel said as she

immediately snatched up a pair of oven gloves and hurried over to the Aga.

Shadow felt a little confused as he watched her open the heavy oven door and waft away the heat. Of all the emotions he was expecting to encounter, her breezy cheerfulness wasn't one of them. However, he decided to carry on with his planned line of questioning regardless. He cleared his throat.

"Firstly, Mrs Campbell, I would like to say how sorry Sergeant Chang and I both are for the loss of Alfred and Chloe. This must be a very difficult time for you and your family."

Annabel carefully took a golden-brown apple pie out of the oven and deftly slid it on to a waiting plate.

"Thank you for your sympathy, Chief Inspector, but Alfred and I had been divorced for over fifteen years." She paused holding a knife in mid-air. "I don't like to speak ill of the dead, Chief Inspector, but my ex-husband was not a kind man." She cut a large slice of the steaming hot pie and placed it on to a smaller plate. "And Chloe, well, she wasn't part of our family for very long. She was a sweet enough girl, I suppose, even if she could be a little flighty. Now if you gentlemen would excuse me, I'll be back in a jiffy. Oh, and do help yourselves."

She nodded at the remaining pie before she hurried through an archway, carrying the plate, with the three boisterous dogs at her heel. Jimmy exhaled loudly.

"Well, so far we haven't learnt much, except Mrs C senior is clearly an excellent baker," he said, leaning forward to sniff the pie in appreciation. His hand reached towards the knife.

"Don't you dare," growled Shadow. "And I think you'll find Mrs Campbell is also well practised in the art of understatement."

"Chief?"

"Allow me to translate my mother's words for you, Sergeant," said a deep voice behind them. "My father was a cruel, selfish bully and Chloe only cared about having a good time, no matter who she hurt along the way."

The two detectives spun round in surprise to find a tall man probably in his late twenties standing in the doorway. He was wearing ripped jeans and a black T-shirt. His blond hair was shaved at the sides, but long on top and tied back. He had his mother's bright blue eyes and Shadow noticed a tattoo of an eagle on each of his folded forearms. Shadow thought he had seen him before but couldn't remember where. The young man stepped forward and held out his hand.

"I'm Daniel Campbell, by the way. Son of Alfred and once husband of Chloe."

Shadow and Jimmy both shook his outstretched hand.

"I would offer you our condolences, Mr Campbell, but it sounds like I would be wasting my breath," said Shadow, taking in Dan's expressionless face.

"Don't get me wrong, Chief Inspector, I'd never wish

anyone dead, but if you were to ask me am I sorry the two of them are out of our lives? Then no, I am not."

Shadow nodded. He had to admire the young man's honesty.

"Can I ask when you last saw them both?"

"I saw Alfred when he was on the stage opening the festival, along with half the city, I expect."

"And Chloe?"

Dan's eyes flickered over to the archway his mother had disappeared through before he answered. "Last night too. I spoke to her briefly in her tent after she had finished doing that stupid fortune-telling thing."

"Can I ask what the two of you spoke about?"

"Our annulment." He paused, his face and voice showing no emotion. "But that all seems like a waste of time now. The only one who benefitted was the lawyer."

As he spoke, Shadow remember when he'd seen him before. It was the previous evening. He had been arguing with Martin Plunkett, the solicitor. At that moment, Annabel bustled back into the kitchen.

"Oh, there you are, Dan. Have you offered our guests a cup of tea?" she asked, beginning to fill a large stainless-steel kettle. "Do you take milk and sugar, Chief Inspector? Sergeant Chang?"

Out of the corner of his eye, Shadow could see Jimmy was ready to respond, so he replied quickly. "That's quite all right, Mrs Campbell, please don't trouble yourself. Although

I did want to ask you when you last saw Alfred and Chloe?"

Annabel carried the kettle over to the Aga and placed it on one of the cat-free hobs.

"Last night at the festival," she replied, "but I didn't speak to either of them. I was selling bread at one of the stalls and Dan was in charge of the beer tent. We finished when everyone moved off to St George's Field, and then we both went to watch the longboat race."

"I see, and is it just the two of you who live here?" Shadow was wondering where both the slice of apple pie and the three noisy dogs had vanished to. Annabel and Dan exchanged a brief look before she answered.

"No, Will, my younger son, lives here too."

"Would it be possible to speak with him?"

Annabel hesitated for a second before she replied. "I'll take you through to see him, Chief Inspector, but I must warn you he is quite upset, so I'd appreciate it if you didn't ask him too many questions."

"Of course," agreed Shadow, interested to see at least one member of the family who was grieving.

Annabel led Shadow and Jimmy through the archway, and down another corridor, into a room with two large tartan sofas and prints of farmyard animals on the walls. There was a roaring fire in the grate and the television was showing cartoons. Curled up on one of the sofas was a boy who looked about seventeen. He had dark curly hair and soft brown eyes that were damp with tears. The two terriers were on the sofa next to him and the whippet was slumped at his feet. There was also a pile of soft toys at the end of the sofa. The apple pie on his plate remained untouched and he was holding an old teddy bear tightly to his chest.

"Will," said Annabel gently, "there are two policemen here to see you. This is Mr Shadow and Mr Chang."

The boy looked up and a tear rolled down his cheek. "Are you here about Dad?" he asked.

Shadow knelt down so he was on a level with him. "Hello, Will," he began softly, while still noticing there was a bandage on the hand Will had tucked under his arm. "That's right, we are trying to find out what happened to him. Did you see your dad last night?"

Will nodded as he brushed another tear away with the back of his hand.

"In St Sampson's Square?" Shadow probed gently and Will nodded again. "And then did you go and watch the longboat race?"

This time Will gave his head a firm shake. "No, I went to see the falcon."

The creases on Shadow's forehead deepened. He was puzzled. Did he mean the Falcon Tap, a popular pub on Micklegate? From his build it was possible he was over eighteen and legally allowed to go drinking, but he seemed much younger.

"He means the peregrine falcon that's nesting on the top of the Minster, Chief Inspector," explained Annabel, who was hovering close by. "Will spends hours there watching them with his binoculars, don't you, love?"

"I think they've started flying at night because of all the street lights," replied Will in between loud sniffs.

"Really? Well, that sounds very interesting. You make sure to let me know if you see them. Is your hand sore?"

"Oh, he's always getting into some scrape or other," answered Annabel quickly. "He's the most accident-prone person I've ever met."

Will smiled weakly and Shadow decided not to bother the young man any further.

"Thank you very much for your help, Will."

Shadow patted him on the arm as he rose to his feet. As they left the room, Jimmy gave Will a smile and a friendly wave, but the boy just buried his face back into his teddy bear. When they returned to the kitchen, Shadow turned to Annabel.

"Was he very close to his father?"

But before she could answer, Dan stepped in.

"Will loves everyone, Chief Inspector. It is impossible for him to see the bad in people. He might be a bit slower than most, but what he's lacking intellectually, he makes up for in emotional intelligence. He's got a bigger heart than the rest of us all put together. Not that Alfred cared about that, he practically disowned Will because he's a bit different. He thought it reflected badly on him. How could the great Alfred Campbell have a son who was less than perfect? Will treated Alfred like a hero, but he just made fun of him and teased him."

Dan's eyes flashed angrily as he spoke. It was the first time Shadow had seen him show any emotion since they had arrived.

"What was your brother's relationship with Chloe like?" he asked.

"I introduced him to her not long after we got married. When Chloe first met Will, she thought he was funny and teased him like Alfred did." He shook his head in disgust. "I knew then I had made a terrible mistake and that was before she'd even set her sights on Alfred. The two of them were made for each other." Dan almost spat out the words.

Shadow turned back to Annabel. "You said that you and Alfred divorced fifteen years ago?"

"Yes, Will was only a toddler. The boys and I stayed here after the divorce, but Alfred sold the land for development. It was such a shame. Will adores all animals. He would have loved living on a proper farm and helping out. That didn't matter to Alfred. Once he was sure all the treasure had been dug up, he was only interested in selling the land to the highest bidder."

"So where did he live?" asked Jimmy, who, as ever, had been busy noting everything down.

"He bought the Old Bonding Warehouse down by the river and developed it into flats; of course, he kept the best for himself: the duplex."

Shadow nodded. He knew the Old Bonding Warehouse well; it was close to where he moored *Florence*. Dan reached up on top of the dresser and collected a large box of tissues.

"I'm going to check on Will. Goodbye, Chief Inspector, Sergeant, and good luck." With that he stalked through the archway. The two detectives and Annabel watched him go.

"Please don't judge Dan too harshly, Chief Inspector," she said softly. "Chloe and his father treated him very cruelly."

"I understand the two of them were in a relationship. That can't have been an easy situation."

Annabel slumped down into one of the chairs, gesturing the detectives should do the same. Shadow thought she suddenly looked very tired compared to the bright and breezy woman who had opened the door.

"Chloe arrived in the city about ten months ago. She got a job working in the bar Dan runs – they always need extra staff over the busy Christmas period. She was a very pretty, vivacious girl. The two of them spent a lot of time working together and, well, one thing led to another. After a few months, Chloe told Dan she was in the family way and Dan has always been one to face up to his responsibilities. So, he whisked her up to Gretna Green without telling anyone and they returned as man and wife."

"Chloe was pregnant?" interrupted Jimmy, flicking back through his notes. Shadow scowled over at him. It didn't matter how many times he lectured his sergeant on never asking questions until the witness had finished speaking, Jimmy was incapable of holding his tongue. Sophie would definitely have said if she'd found Chloe was expecting and it was unlikely they would have forgotten a detail like that. Meanwhile, Annabel was shaking her head ruefully.

"A week after the wedding, Chloe announced she had made a mistake – she wasn't pregnant after all. She made it sound like she had simply misplaced her car keys or caught the wrong train, not wrecked Dan's life! 'Silly me!' she said." Annabel paused, as if needing to compose herself before she went on. "About the same time Alfred returned from the Channel Islands. He often goes down to his place there during the winter months. As soon as they met, Chloe quickly set about working her charm on him and Alfred – well, he always enjoyed the company of pretty women. By then, as Dan said, he had seen Chloe for what she really was. His heart wasn't broken, but his pride certainly took a bruising. As you say, Chief Inspector, it was not an easy situation."

CHAPTER FOUR

Across 2 (8 letters)
A bat you can't trust hides in this layer

S HADOW AND JIMMY left Battlefield Farm and drove back towards the city centre.

"What do you think, Chief? Surely Dan must be a suspect. He could have strangled Chloe then gone and stuck that sword in his father. He even admitted his life would be better without them. He also said he was pleased to be rid of Chloe."

Shadow had started to grind his teeth. He wanted a few quiet moments with his own thoughts instead of having to listen to his sergeant's abridged version of the conversations that had just occurred.

"This may come as a shock to you, Sergeant," he said sarcastically, "but sometimes people don't tell the police the truth."

They spent the rest of the journey in silence except for the occasional shout of "Brake!" or "Careful!" from Shadow. He kept thinking about Dan and Will and how cruel Alfred had been to them both and yet how different their reactions to his death were. When they arrived back at the station car park Jimmy's phone began bleeping.

"Anything?" asked Shadow.

Jimmy shook his head. "Forensics. I asked them to check the blood that was found on the last broken window – the one at the toy shop – but there's no match on the database."

Shadow raised his eyes heavenward, but before he could begin berating his sergeant, Kevin MacNab suddenly appeared in front of them. Shadow got the distinct feeling he had been lurking in the car park and waiting for them to come back.

"Ah the wanderers return!" said Kevin with a self-satisfied smile. "Two unexplained deaths in less than twenty-four hours, the Viking Festival, one of the highlights of the city's tourism calendar cancelled, surely the chief investigating officer had something to say to my readers?"

"No comment," replied Shadow automatically, but the journalist was not about to be put off this time.

"Wait now, Chief Inspector, let me finish, hear me out. In return for an interview—" he took an envelope out of his pocket and waved it slowly in front of Shadow's face "—what I have in here is a disc of the vlog I was making about the Viking Festival. I'm sure you remember seeing me there last night. This disc contains full footage from the evening. Who knows, maybe you'll even be able to spot the murderer." His expression was growing smugger by the second as he continued wafting the disc slowly back and forth, a few inches from

Shadow's nose. Too slowly. Jimmy's long arm suddenly reached out and snatched the envelope from Kevin's hand.

"Hey!" cried Kevin in outrage. "I want something in return for that!"

"Fine! In return we won't charge you with attempting to withhold evidence." Shadow smiled easily.

"Or trying to bribe a police officer," agreed Jimmy with a grin.

"And you get a sense of satisfaction knowing you've done your civic duty," continued Shadow.

Kevin glowered at them both for a moment, his face turning red beneath his freckles, before he stomped away without another word. Jimmy chuckled as he watched him go. Shadow turned to him.

"What is a vlog anyway?" he asked.

"Don't worry, it's not important, Chief," sighed Jimmy. When they first started working together, Jimmy used to try to explain new technology to his boss. However, as Shadow still hardly even bothered to read his emails and text messages, Jimmy no longer troubled him with anything more advanced.

"Right, well in that case, you have a look at that disc and find out if it does contain anything useful. I'm off to get some lunch."

HE LEFT JIMMY behind and strode out of the station car park and across St Helen's Square. The rain had eased, and the sun was trying its best to break through the grey clouds. Outside the police station's main entrance several reporters and a camera crew were waiting. No doubt hoping for a quote about the investigation. He put his head down and kept walking towards Stonegate. He turned right into the first pub he came to. It happened to be the Punch Bowl, which was known to serve one of the best steak and ale pies in the city. Shadow was ravenous after having only a muffin for breakfast, and smelling Annabel's delicious baking certainly hadn't helped.

He ordered a pie and a pint of Theakston's Old Peculier, then settled into a seat by the window. He took a sip of his pint and unfolded his crossword, but it was no good. Thoughts about the case kept getting in the way of the clues. He contemplated the two murders, if that was what they were. There was no doubt in his mind the two deaths were connected, but he wondered if it could possibly be a combination of murder and suicide.

Annabel had described Chloe as flighty and Shadow had seen for himself that she was vivacious, flirty even. What if Alfred, who by all accounts was a proud man, had taken exception to his young girlfriend's flirting, returned to her tent, and killed her in a fit of jealousy. Then, filled with remorse, had taken his own life. But why go all the way back to Ragnar's Palace to commit suicide, and why not kill Chloe with the sword too?

Shadow's pie arrived and as he took his first mouthful, he shook his head. From what he already knew about Alfred, it did not sound like remorse was an emotion he often experienced. If he had killed Chloe, he had the impression Alfred was the type to make a run for it. As he continued to eat his excellent lunch, Shadow's thoughts drifted to Dan and what his disagreement with the solicitor could have been about. Had Plunkett been acting for Chloe? If so, what was there to argue about?

WITH A NOW-FULL stomach, Shadow returned to the station in a much better mood than when he had left. After dodging the waiting press by going through the side entrance, he found Jimmy looking at a screen showing a frozen image of Kevin MacNab's face.

"Please tell me you haven't been staring at him all this time?" Shadow grimaced.

Jimmy laughed. "Yes, but I had to turn the volume down. The sound of his voice was doing my head in. By the way, Sophie called. She has put the time of Chloe's death at between eight o'clock and eleven o'clock. She said sorry not to be more accurate, but as the body was outside all night, that's the best she can do. She also said – and this is the really interesting bit – the cause of Chloe's death wasn't asphyxiation, but a head trauma. Sophie thinks she was either pushed or fell and hit her head on the candelabra. There were traces of wax in the back of her hair."

Shadow stared at his deputy in disbelief. "Then why make it look like she's been strangled when she's dead already?" He frowned. "It doesn't make sense."

"I don't know, Chief." Jimmy shrugged. "But I also took a call from Donaldson. He wasn't very happy about speaking to me instead of you. There was talk of organ grinders and monkeys, but he has ruled out suicide for Alfred. He said, and I quote, he wouldn't waste his breath trying to explain the finer details to me, but basically for the length of his arm and the angle of the sword entering the body it was all wrong to be self-inflicted."

"He was as charming as ever then," snorted Shadow, but at least he now knew he was right to think Alfred's death was unlikely to be suicide. He turned his attention back to the screen. "What is MacNab actually doing?"

"He's made a video of the Viking Festival and added his commentary to post online. I think it's known as trying to raise his media profile, Chief."

"That's all we need! Has he given us anything of any use?"

"Yes, but first let me show you this." Jimmy began spooling back through Kevin's footage. He paused and then played the disc. Kevin was in the frame speaking earnestly as Vikings and tourists milled around him, but over his shoulder, grinning and waving at the camera, was Will Campbell. As soon as Kevin realised, he turned and shooed him away. Shadow and Jimmy both laughed as they watched.

"I just thought you'd like to see him looking happy, Chief – the poor kid," explained Jimmy with a sympathetic shake of his head. He now fast-forwarded to the first image he had been studying. Again, Kevin was looking seriously down the lens, but now it was dark, and the square was almost deserted. Shadow thought it must have been an hour or so after both he and the Great Heathen Army had departed. Most of the tents had already closed for the night. As Jimmy zoomed in to an area in the background, it became clear he was focusing on Chloe's tent, or at least the last third of it. The rest was out of shot.

"Now look closely, Chief," he said.

Shadow fumbled for his glasses, leant forward, and peered at the screen as Jimmy pressed play. After a couple of seconds, someone walked very quickly out of the rear entrance of the tent. It was almost impossible to make out who it was in the darkness. It was clearly a tall man with chin-length hair, but that description fitted half the people at the festival. However, as the figure passed by one of the flaming torches, they raised their hand to rake through their hair and as their sleeve fell back from their arm. Jimmy pressed pause. Caught in the light, the distinctive tattoo of an eagle was clearly visible.

"Dan," murmured Shadow.

"That's right!" agreed Jimmy. "And if you look at the old clock on the wall of Marks and Spencer…" Jimmy tapped his pen on the area of the screen where the clock face was visible. It was showing the time eight twenty-five. "I know he said he spoke to her that night…"

"But now we've got evidence showing him leaving the tent, that fits in with the window for time of death," finished Shadow. "I don't suppose you can remember if you saw him at the longboat race?" he asked hopefully. Dan certainly had enough reason to want Chloe and Alfred dead. If they could place him near the St George's Field encampment too, they might be making progress.

"I was thinking about that, Chief," replied Jimmy as he fished his mobile phone out of his jacket pocket. "I can't remember seeing him exactly, but I did take quite a few photos that night. Look what I found."

Shadow squinted at the small screen as Jimmy began scrolling through the pictures. He couldn't help noticing that Sophie appeared in quite a few of them. One also showed Alfred standing in the middle of Skeldergate Bridge.

"When was that one taken?" asked Shadow.

"At the beginning of the race. Alfred started it off."

Shadow nodded and Jimmy continued to scroll before finally stopping at the image he wanted.

"You see, Chief, each longboat was sponsored by a local business. Plunkett's Solicitors, a couple of local breweries, Asgard's bar, who won, incidentally," Jimmy explained. "You see in this one everyone is cheering the winning team. As manager of the bar, Dan is there as well. Not exactly the picture of happiness, is he?"

Shadow looked at the young man's expression. One word came to mind: *troubled*. In a crowd of happy, smiling faces, his grim stare certainly stood out.

"What time did you take that photo?"

Jimmy tapped on the image a couple of times and looked up. "Eight fifty-six, Chief."

"Right," said Shadow, "well, it might only be circumstantial evidence, but let's go and speak to him again. Find out where he is."

DAN WAS AT work. As Shadow and Jimmy had already discovered, he ran Asgard, the Viking-themed café bar. It stood on Coppergate, alongside the Daneholm museum and shop, and Valhalla nightclub, which at this time of day was closed. Alfred had certainly cornered the market when it came to all things Norse in the city. His Viking-orientated empire dominated the entire street. Everyone was catered for, from a young schoolboy looking for his own helmet and wooden sword, to a hen party wanting to dress up as shield maidens and have a night out with a difference.

"You go into the museum and see if you can find out anything there," said Shadow. "I'll go and speak to Dan again."

Jimmy headed to the museum entrance, his digital note-book at the ready, while Shadow stepped through the huge wooden doors into Asgard. Inside it looked like a larger more permanent version of Ragnar's Palace, although the ceiling was much higher. Two roaring fires burned at either end of the room and the walls were decorated with swords, painted shields, and axes.

The bar was busy despite, or perhaps because of the festi-val being cancelled. A large group of Norwegian tourists sat on wooden chairs and benches draped with faux fur covers. A few very tall men dressed in Viking costumes stood at the long wooden bar loudly telling jokes and drinking from metal tankards. Dan himself was behind the bar. He looked a little wary when he saw Shadow approach, but his tone was pleasant enough when he spoke.

"Afternoon, Chief Inspector, I didn't expect to see you again so soon. Can I interest you in a pint? A Hardrada's Revenge or a Thor's Thunder maybe?"

Shadow surveyed the pump handles suspiciously. "It's not mead, is it?"

"Hell no! That's terrible stuff!" Dan laughed. "Although we do have bottles of Freya's Nectar for any tourists who want to sample it."

"All right then, I'll try a pint of Hardrada's Revenge."

"I take it this isn't a social call?" Dan enquired as he pulled the pint.

"No," Shadow replied. "There's video footage of you leaving your ex-wife's tent at the time she was killed."

"So?" Dan shrugged, placing the tankard in front of Shadow. "I already told you I spoke with her."

"Cheers," said Shadow, lifting the tankard.

"*Skol*," responded Dan, raising his own pint from behind the bar.

"Can you tell me more about the conversation you had?" Shadow took his first tentative sip from the tankard. It was surprisingly good.

Dan shrugged again and began wiping down the bar. "Only stuff about the annulment. She got upset and accused me of being jealous, but honestly, Chief Inspector, that is the last thing I felt. Chloe could be a real drama queen. I thought it was easier if I just left."

"You described your father as being cruel?"

"He was," insisted Dan, then seeing Shadow was expecting more: "Okay, let me give you an example. Winston, the dog you saw sleeping by the Aga – he isn't deaf because he's old; he's been that way for years, thanks to Alfred. He bought Winston because he wanted a Labrador to take shooting with his new posh friends, but Winston was gun-shy. To Alfred that meant he was useless, so he shut him in a shed and kept firing a twelve-bore into the air at close range. He said he thought it would cure him. It didn't of course; it just terrified the poor dog and sent him deaf."

Shadow winced at the story. He'd always liked dogs.

He'd had a Labrador when he was a boy and could never understand anyone wanting to treat them badly.

"You implied Alfred didn't treat your brother much better?"

Dan stopped wiping the bar. His jaw tensed and he looked Shadow straight in the eye.

"Like Mum told you, Will loves animals, all animals. These horns and skulls—" he pointed behind the bar where several were nailed to the wall "—they are fakes, made of resin, but Dad used to tell Will they were real. He said he'd gone out and hunted and killed them himself. He'd go on and on until he had Will in tears."

"And yet Will's the only one who seems to be mourning Alfred's death."

"That's Will for you," replied Dan with a sad shake of his head.

"Who inherits this place now? Did Alfred leave a will?"

"As far as I know, he left everything to me."

Dan's voice and face were as devoid of expression as they had been earlier in the day. Then, he didn't seem like a man who had been told his father had died; now, he didn't look or sound like someone who was due to inherit millions.

"How do you feel about that?" asked Shadow.

"To be honest, Chief Inspector, right now I just feel like selling up. Getting rid of the whole damn lot. The museum, the club, this place, everything. Since Dad found that treasure, it's caused nothing but trouble."

"If you feel that strongly why stay here? It can't have been easy working for your father, feeling the way you do about him."

"I couldn't leave, Chief Inspector. I had to stick around to help with Will and for poor Mum." He nodded towards the far corner of the room.

Shadow turned his head. He hadn't notice before, but Annabel was sitting with Edward Bennington at a small table by the fire. The two of them looked quite out of place sharing a pot of tea and a plate of shortbread amongst the beer-swilling young Viking fans. Shadow thanked Dan and walked over to their table.

"May I join you?" he asked. They both looked up in surprise. They had clearly been engrossed in their conversation.

"Of course, Chief Inspector," replied Edward, pulling out a chair for him. Shadow sat down and noticed Edward was now wearing his half-moon spectacles and wristwatch. He thought Annabel looked pale and tired compared to the bright cheerful woman he had met a few hours ago.

"I understand the Viking Festival has been cancelled?" he began. Edward nodded his head sadly.

"I'm afraid so, Chief Inspector. Out of respect for Alfred and Chloe, you understand. I just hope everyone isn't too disappointed. It's the first time it's been cancelled in over twenty years."

"Did you make the decision, Mr Bennington?"

Edward looked quite shocked at the thought. "Oh no,

Chief Inspector, dear me no, at least not just me – it was the board's decision." He paused as if he was realising something for the first time. "Although with Alfred gone, the board is only Martin Plunkett and myself. We consulted Annabel too, naturally – but really, Chief Inspector, Alfred *was* the festival and with him gone…" Edward trailed off and Annabel took over.

"It was fun in the early days, Chief Inspector," she said, sounding wistful. "Back then it was about a few local families getting together. Some were experts, like Edward here, but the rest of us simply enjoyed dressing up. The children would run around with their swords and shields. These days though, it has become all about the money. Alfred getting businesses to sponsor everything. It's become, so, oh what's the word?"

"Corporate?" suggested Shadow.

She smiled weakly at him. "Yes, Chief Inspector. Exactly. Corporate and so busy."

"We used to have a wonderful time re-enacting all the Viking legends, didn't we?" reminisced Edward. "Alfred was Thor, I was Odin, and you were Freya. Annabel's quite the actress, you know, Chief Inspector."

"Now, Edward, stop that – you're embarrassing me." Annabel laughed. "We all used to be in a local am-dram group, Chief Inspector. In fact, that's how I met Alfred."

"I remember that year," added Edward. "It was our production of *Oliver!* Alfred played Bill Sykes."

"Naturally!" interjected Annabel.

"And Annabel was the most wonderful Nancy."

Annabel flapped her hands at him. "Oh, do stop it, Edward. Chief Inspector Shadow doesn't want to hear all this nonsense, and besides," she said, suddenly looking rather sad, "it all seems a very long time ago now."

Shadow smiled sympathetically, before turning back to Edward. "Mr Bennington, can I ask whose phone you used to call us when you found Alfred?"

"Yes, it was Martin's. I don't mind telling you I was in a bit of a flap. I went to look for someone to help and as luck would have it, Martin was the first person I stumbled across."

"Was he far away?"

"Oh no, he was standing right outside Ragnar's Palace, Chief Inspector."

Shadow thanked them both for their time and stood up to leave as the inebriated Norwegians loudly began chanting *skol* repeatedly as they downed their beers.

WHEN SHADOW STEPPED outside Asgard, it was already almost dark. The street felt eerily quiet after leaving behind the noisy customers in the bar. Edward and Annabel seemed very fond of each other. He wondered if it was possible they were more than friends. A moment later, Jimmy appeared from the museum doorway.

"Anything?" asked Shadow.

"Firstly, Chief, I got a text to say they traced the phone that made the 999 call. It's registered to Martin Plunkett."

"I know, I know," replied Shadow, waving his hand dismissively. "Anything else?"

"Well," began Jimmy, tapping open his ever-present notebook, "they are all a bit shell-shocked obviously, Chief. Altogether, there are six members of staff, two full-time, four part-time…"

Shadow held up his hand to stop him as he wrinkled his nose in disgust. "For crying out loud! What is that terrible smell?" he asked.

Jimmy sniffed the arm of his leather jacket self-consciously. "I think it might be me, Chief. You see in the museum they have created this Viking village and it smells like it did back then and, well, they didn't have a proper sewerage system, did they? The staff warned me it might linger."

Shadow took a step back. "In that case, unless you are going to tell me someone at the museum has written a signed confession, I think we'll call it a day. Go home and for heaven's sake, have a shower!"

HALF AN HOUR later, Shadow was sitting at his usual window table at Catania. It was another of his favourite Italian restaurants on Goodramgate and was popular with tourists and families alike. Red and green metal chairs surrounded round white marble-topped tables. Framed vintage posters of Venice, Florence, and Rome lined the walls and Italian pop music played through the speakers.

Shadow was enjoying his evening meal of medaglioni di manzo even more than usual after such a disappointing supper the previous night. When he had finished, he pushed his knife and fork together with a satisfied sigh. He took a large sip of his Barolo, leaned back in his chair, and gazed out of the window while he pondered the case.

He had a wonderful view across College Green to the floodlit Minster's magnificent east window. It was the largest medieval stained-glass window in England and looking at it usually gave him a sense of peace and perspective.

However, tonight it merely made him focus on one aspect of the case that was particularly bothering him. It was how peaceful both bodies had looked. In all his years in the police, he had never seen murder scenes like them. Apart from the dead bodies themselves, there was no sign of violence at either site.

His eyes drifted away from the window and he noticed there was someone sitting on the bench on College Green. It was cold and dark outside, but they were nevertheless sitting there, looking up at the Minster. Who on earth could it be? He strained his eyes and realised, with a start, it was Will

Campbell. He was wrapped up in a hat and scarf, but it was definitely him.

At that moment, the lights of the restaurant were dimmed and the opening chords of "Happy Birthday" struck up. Shadow turned to see Gino, the restaurant owner, carrying a cake covered in candles over to a little boy, who was out celebrating with his family. His father was beaming proudly as he dashed round the table with his camera, trying to get the perfect angle of the excited birthday boy before he blew out all the candles. Shadow politely joined in the round of applause along with the other diners.

He could barely remember his own father, who had died when Shadow was three years old. He had been a village policeman. One night he had gone to investigate poaching on the local estate and been shot – by mistake or otherwise, nobody was sure. Shadow and his mother had left the village and moved to York so she could find work in one of the chocolate factories. She had never really forgiven Shadow for following his father into the police.

"How could you, John?" she'd said when he'd first broached the subject. "How could you be so cruel?" She had refused to discuss the matter any further or to attend his passing-out ceremony at Hendon. His grandparents on his father's side had telegrammed their congratulations and told him how proud they were. However, they were both too old to leave the farm and travel down to London, so he had graduated alone.

Shadow took another long drink of wine. He hadn't thought about his father in years, but this case had made him wonder what their relationship might have been like. He hoped very much it wouldn't have been like Alfred Campbell's was with his two sons. There was Dan, who couldn't even bring himself to call Alfred Dad and felt humiliated by his actions. Then Will, who hero-worshipped his father, while Alfred only bullied and teased him. To Shadow, Dan was a bit of a conundrum. He had strong motives for wanting to kill both Alfred and Chloe, yet Shadow was inclined to believe everything he had told him.

When Shadow turned back to the window, he found Will had been joined by two others. One was clearly Dan and the other a tall young woman with her pale blonde hair tied into a high ponytail. From their body language, it looked like they were trying to encourage Will to go with them. After a few moments of Will pointing up at the Minster, he finally gave in. He stood up, hugged his brother, and the three of them walked away down Goodramgate together. Shadow watched them go, finished his wine, and called for the bill.

He stepped outside into the bracing night air, turned up the collar of his wax jacket against the chill wind, and stuck his hands deep in his pockets. As he was about to set off, he heard a high-pitched screech above his head. He looked up and sure enough, there swooping above the Minster was the peregrine falcon. He smiled to himself. Perhaps Will knew more than everyone gave him credit for.

CHAPTER FIVE

Across 7 (7 letters)
The scent at the start of this femme is pure

THE NEXT DAY dawned bright and sunny. It was a perfect autumn morning with the leaves on the trees by the riverbank turning gold and red. After a lie-in, Shadow strolled along the towpath neatly sidestepping the geese, who were refusing to move and making life difficult for the Sunday morning cyclists.

Shadow was pleasantly surprised when Julie came to take his breakfast order. She didn't normally work on a Sunday. A few moments later, she returned with his pot of tea then hovered by his table looking a little self-conscious.

"I hope you don't mind me asking," she began tentatively, "but I just wondered how Annabel was coping with everything that's going on?"

Shadow looked up. For a second, he was stumped. They very occasionally made small talk, but it was usually restricted to the weather, never his work.

"Oh, you know, bearing up I think," he replied. "How do you know her?"

"She was in my sister's year at school. Joanne always said Annabel was the class clown. She used to have the whole class in stitches when she played tricks on the teachers or did impressions of them. She always looks quite down when I see her these days, but then I suppose none of us are as happy as we were back then. What do they say? School days are the best days of your lives."

Shadow smiled politely as she left, but personally he thought that sentiment couldn't be more wrong. He had been happy enough at primary school with Maggie and all the other local children, but that had all changed when he'd won a scholarship to a boarding school down in Hampshire. His time there had been nothing short of miserable.

After enjoying a late and much more leisurely breakfast than the previous day, Shadow headed to the station and straight up to the incident room. A team of uniformed officers were working their way through the mountain of statements that had been collected from the Vikings and tourists after Alfred's body had been discovered. They were also fielding calls from members of the public with information or concerns. Jimmy was busy speaking on the telephone. Shadow waved over to him, but he signalled back that there was nothing yet to report.

Shadow left the station and made the short walk across Lendal to the Judge's Lodging. The elegant red-brick building surrounded by wrought-iron railings had once been the temporary home of visiting judges when they came to attend the city's assizes. It was now a boutique hotel, with a public bar in the cellar. Shadow walked down the worn, old stone steps.

The bar had a cosy feeling with its low-beamed ceiling and portraits of distinguished judges who had visited lining the walls. It almost felt like being in someone's living room. Shadow had arranged to meet his old friend Sergeant George Hedley from the police records office there. He found a small wooden table by the log fire, with leather armchairs either side. A few moments after he had taken his seat, George arrived too. Shadow stood up and shook his hand.

"Good of you to meet me on a Sunday, George."

"Not at all. Carol's holding a coffee morning at ours, so I was pleased to have an excuse to escape." George grinned.

"Pint?"

"Best make it an orange juice – I'm babysitting later. Harry's just learnt to walk, so he's keeping me on my toes."

Shadow smiled. George was an extremely proud grandfather.

"Sounds like you've got your hands full."

"I wouldn't have it any other way, John."

Shadow returned to their table a few moments later with his pint of Black Sheep and a fruit juice for George.

"So," began George, "I take it this is about the Alf Campbell case? I think you might have your work cut out with this one, John. The suspects must be queuing up around the corner."

"He really was a nasty piece of work then?" asked Shadow. So far, he had only heard from people who were closely connected to Alfred. It would be good to get a neutral point of view. George had lived in York all his life and had an almost encyclopaedic memory. There was very little that had happened in the city over the last forty years or so that he couldn't tell you about. He frowned and shook his head now.

"Oh, don't get me wrong, Alfred could be charming when he wanted to be, but there are plenty in York who have seen his other side."

"What can you tell me about Edward Bennington? He doesn't strike me as the sort of man Alfred would have had a lot of time for, let alone put him on the management board of the Viking Festival."

George took a sip of his juice, then settled back in his armchair. With his glasses perched on the end of his nose, he looked like a professor about to give a history lecture instead of a policeman.

"Well, that's really where it all began. It must have happened before you came back to York. Alfred inherited Battlefield Farm in Fulford, from a great-uncle, I believe. It had been quite a successful pig farm, but Alfred wasn't interested in keeping it going. The life of a farmer was far too much like hard work for him. What he really wanted to do was sell the land for development, but he couldn't get planning permission because technically it was classed as a site of historic interest."

"Why historic interest?" asked Shadow, half wishing he had brought Jimmy and his electronic notebook.

"The farm was where the Battle of Fulford was meant to have happened back in 1066, hence the name of the farm."

Shadow's forehead creased as he recalled the history of the Norman Conquest from his school days. He could still hear the words of his teacher, a veteran of World War II, proudly declaring, *"We haven't been invaded for over a thousand years, boys. The Spanish and their Armada, Napoleon and the French, even the Germans under Hitler, have all tried and all failed. Not since William the Conqueror in 1066 have foreign invaders succeeded in their quest."*

"In 1066?" Shadow queried. "I thought that was the year for the battles of Stamford Bridge and Hastings."

"Fulford was before them both – that's why nobody re-members it," explained George. "The Vikings actually won at Fulford, but went on to lose at Stamford Bridge. Anyway, back to Edward Bennington. As you probably know he's a bit of a Viking nut, he even went over to Norway to learn more about them. Now, local legend had it that the Vikings buried their treasure at Fulford to keep it safe before the Battle of Stamford Bridge. As we know, Harald Hardrada's army was defeated by Harold Godwinson and the Vikings fled."

"Without collecting their treasure?"

"Exactly! Well, for Edward locating the treasure became

a bit of an obsession. He spent hours and hours studying old maps and writings from that era. He was convinced he had worked out where the treasure was buried, and it happened to be in a field on Alfred's farm. Thinking Alfred was a friend, he told him all about it, but Alfred refused to give him permission to look for the treasure. Instead, he bought himself a metal detector and a spade and…"

"Found the Fulford Hoard," finished Shadow, before taking a sip of his pint.

George nodded. "And became a millionaire. Technically, I suppose you could argue, as it was his land, he didn't cheat Edward, but most people thought it was still pretty underhand."

"And yet Edward was happy to serve on the board of the festival?"

"Not just the festival. He's on the board of the Daneholm museum too. In fact, I think he designed most of it. I expect he thought it was better than nothing and at least he was involved with the artefacts in some way. For Edward it was always about the historic, not the monetary value of the treasure. From Alfred's point of view, it looked good to have someone with Edward's academic qualifications and depth of knowledge on the board. Let's face it though, John, there may have been three names on the board, but when it came to making decisions, there was only one boss. What Alfred said, went."

Shadow sat and considered the farmhouse in Fulford,

now surrounded by new houses.

"And Alfred did eventually get planning permission. Was that because it had all been excavated?"

George downed the last of his juice and nodded. "Maybe the archaeologists spent a few years digging it all up. But, if you ask me, it was more to do with Alfred's new-found wealth. A case of money talks. Now, I had best make a move, or Carol will be sending out a search party. She complains enough as it is about the time I spend at work."

"You can always blame me," offered Shadow.

George grinned at him. "Don't worry, I do."

The two men shook hands and Shadow thanked George again for his time.

Now he was alone, Shadow mulled over what George had told him as he finished the last of his pint. Edward Bennington seemed mild-mannered enough, but he had been treated badly by Alfred. Could feelings of resentment have been building up all these years? Were they enough to make him a killer?

When Shadow stepped back outside, blinking in the bright sunshine, he almost bumped into Jimmy coming down the steps.

"Are you tracking my phone again?" he asked, suspicious. When the two men had first begun working together, Jimmy used to do this as a way of keeping tabs on Shadow.

"Of course not, Chief, but I spotted George leaving here and thought it was unlikely he would have been drinking alone."

"Very impressive, Sergeant. With those powers of deduction, it's no wonder you're in CID. Why were you looking for me anyway?" Shadow asked as they left the Judge's Lodging and walked back down Lendal.

"We've got Chloe's bag. I thought you'd want to take a look at it before we send it off to forensics, Chief."

"Where did you find it?"

"A guy was down on the Foss fishing first thing this morning. He saw it bobbing about, scooped it out, and handed it in at the reception desk."

"How do you know it's Chloe's? I thought all her ID was in her purse?"

"Well, we don't for sure, Chief," admitted Jimmy, "but it's made of leopard-print fabric – like the purse – and the make-up bag we found inside has the name Chloe on the front, spelt out in gold glitter."

"Fair enough," accepted Shadow.

THE TWO DETECTIVES returned to the station where the bag was waiting for them on Shadow's desk in his office. Shadow frowned as he entered the room. Something was different.

"What's happened to the lighting?" he asked. The place now had a strange whitish glow.

"New energy efficient light bulbs, Chief," explained

Jimmy. "It was the chief constable's idea. She's trying to make the station more environmentally friendly."

"That's all we need," complained Shadow. Although she was based out at Northallerton at the county's police headquarters, the chief constable still often managed to make her presence felt in the city.

Someone had thoughtfully placed a plastic sheet beneath the soggy bag as it was still seeping river water. There were also two pairs of latex gloves. Shadow and Jimmy each put a pair on, knowing that the forensics team would be less than impressed if they contaminated any evidence.

Shadow carefully opened the zip and peered inside. The contents included many of the items he thought had been missing from the fortune-telling tent. There was a hairbrush, comb, set of keys on a keyring shaped like a red stiletto shoe, the cosmetic bag decorated with the name Chloe, and a small gold and crystal atomiser. Nestled at the bottom of the bag was a blue velvet jewellery gift box. Shadow opened it. Inside it was empty, but the letters E T D were printed in gold on the lid. He closed the lid and rummaged further. Finally, he found two mobile phones both with badly smashed screens. The one with a leopard-print cover had to be Chloe's; the larger one, he could only assume was Alfred's.

"Any chance you think we'll be able to retrieve anything from these?" he asked. Jimmy grimaced and shook his head.

"I doubt it, Chief."

Shadow unzipped the bulging cosmetic bag. It was

crammed with tubes, brushes, compacts and all sorts of paraphernalia that appeared quite alien to the two detectives. Shadow put it to one side and picked up the atomiser instead. He unscrewed the lid and a small trickle of pale brown water ran out. Holding it at arm's length, he pressed down the top and a squirt of perfume sprayed out. Shadow and Jimmy both leaned forward and sniffed the air gingerly. The scent was still surprisingly strong despite it being submerged in the Foss for hours.

"It's quite nice, Chief, you know, considering," said Jimmy, sniffing again, but Shadow was frowning. He knew the scent. He had smelt it somewhere before, but where? And then it dawned on him.

"It's the smell from Ragnar's Palace!" he exclaimed.

"Sorry, Chief?"

"When we were looking at Alfred's body there was a strong smell of perfume in the air. This was that perfume."

"Really? Well, then that must mean Chloe was there before or at the time Alfred was murdered. Maybe she witnessed something and was killed so she didn't talk. Or maybe she killed Alfred, and someone murdered her in revenge."

Shadow held up his hand to silence his enthusiastic sergeant before he thought up any more scenarios.

"Let's not get ahead of ourselves," he cautioned. "For all we know, half the women in York could wear this perfume."

He picked up a Post-it Note, ignored the message on it,

folded it in half, sprayed it liberally with the perfume, waved it in the air to dry it, then tucked it into his wallet. He turned back to Jimmy.

"Check with uniform and see if anyone reported seeing Chloe at the longboat race. We already know when she was in the tent with Dan. Then get this lot down to forensics and tell them I want those keys back as soon as possible. I want to know exactly where Chloe had access to. I'll see you back here."

With that Shadow left the station and headed down Coney Street towards a large chemist shop, which he knew would be open on a Sunday. He stepped through the automatic sliding doors and had to blink twice as his eyes grew accustomed to the glaring bright lights and the gleaming white surfaces everywhere. He made his way down the aisles, passing groups of teenage girls squealing and giggling as they experimented with samples of lipsticks and nail varnishes.

The perfume counter was at the far end of the shop. Arranged behind the glass front of the display cabinets was a dizzying array of bottles and boxes, in all manner of shapes, sizes, and colours. Shadow scratched his head as he wondered where he should start, but then a shop assistant seemed to almost magically appear before him. She was a young woman wearing a stark white coat. Her jet-black hair was tied back into a very tight ponytail and behind her green-framed rectangular glasses, all her facial features appeared to have been drawn in, from her bright crimson lips to her angular, black eyebrows.

"May I help you, sir?" she enquired politely.

"Ah, yes I hope so," began Shadow, rooting through his pockets for his wallet, then finally fishing out the folded Post-it Note, as the assistant waited patiently. "I was wondering if you could tell me what this perfume is?"

The young woman looked a little puzzled at his unusual request but took the Post-it and hesitantly held it up to her nose. Recognition registered immediately and a bright smile spread across her face. "Oh yes, it's 'Femme de la Nuit', sir."

Shadow was impressed. "Well done, that was quick. Is it a popular scent?"

"Femme de la Nuit is one of our most exclusive perfumes, sir. A heavy, floral scent with subtle notes of vanilla and sandalwood. Are you thinking of purchasing a gift for a special lady in your life?" the assistant replied as she turned to unlock the cabinet behind her.

Shadow mentally translated *exclusive* to mean *expensive*. "Err yes, my sister," he replied. Shadow was an only child, but he didn't want to startle the unsuspecting girl by telling her he was investigating a murder. The assistant turned back and placed a small black and gold box on the counter in front of Shadow.

"This is the one-hundred-millilitre bottle, sir. Would you like me to gift-wrap it for you?"

Shadow noticed the discreet price tag on the side of the

box. He had to look twice. It was three figures.

"No, that's all right. I'll think about it," he said, quickly. The assistant could barely hide her disappointment.

"We do a fifty-millilitre bottle too, sir," she offered.

Shadow shook his head as he began to back away. "Thank you very much for your help," he said as he gave her an apologetic wave.

BACK AT THE station, Jimmy was waiting for him by the window in his office.

"Anything to report?"

"Nothing much I'm afraid, Chief. No sightings of Chloe at the boat race and I checked the photos I took that night, but there was no sign of her. Forensics aren't very hopeful of finding any evidence from the handbag – too much water damage apparently – but they said we could have the keys back tomorrow."

Shadow nodded as he sat down behind his desk and began searching through the drawers for some indigestion tablets. A pint of beer so soon after a full English breakfast may not have been wise.

"Well, I found out the perfume is called 'Femme de la Nuit'," he began, "and judging by its price tag, I think we can be fairly confident it was Chloe in Ragnar's Palace. I can't imagine they sell that many bottles, especially not as gifts."

Yorkshire men were notoriously tight-fisted when it came to parting with their money. Shadow had almost fainted when he had first seen the price they charged for a pint of beer in London. He popped a couple of tablets in his mouth and continued.

"I think it would be too much of a coincidence for another woman with the same scent to have been in there that night. Now, have you got that wretched notebook of yours ready? I'll fill you in on what George told me about Edward Bennington."

Although it was a rhetorical question, Shadow was still surprised when Jimmy didn't respond. He turned around in his chair to see his sergeant staring out of the window across the river. Shadow cleared his throat loudly. "Are you still with me, Sergeant?"

Jimmy turned around apologetically.

"Sorry, Chief, I was just thinking. Sophie's birthday is coming up. Do you think she'd like that perfume?" he asked. Shadow raised an eyebrow and Jimmy hurried on, "You know just because she's a really good friend."

Shadow exhaled loudly and shook his head. "Sergeant, I can't claim to be the most knowledgeable man when it comes to this sort of thing, and it may have been some time since I've bought a gift for a lady, but I do know one thing."

"What's that, Chief?"

"You don't give them perfume worn by a dead woman.

Particularly, if the recipient conducted the post-mortem on said dead woman." He paused before adding, "Even if she is just a really good friend."

Jimmy looked crestfallen. "I didn't think of it like that. You might have a point, Chief. I'll have a rethink."

"Good, you do that. Now, can we get back to the case, please?"

Shadow proceeded to give Jimmy a recap of the history of Edward and Alfred's relationship. When he finished, Jimmy, who had been taking notes, looked up.

"So now we know Edward definitely has a motive for wanting Alfred dead. He must have hated him, and you have got to admit, he was really weird about that old sword."

Shadow nodded in agreement. "Let's go and have another word with Mr Bennington."

THE TWO DETECTIVES stepped out of the office only to find Tom hurrying towards them.

"Chief Inspector, I'm glad I caught you, sir. There's a lady downstairs who wants to speak to someone in CID," he said slightly breathlessly.

"Who is she?" asked Shadow.

"Her name is Miss Treanor, sir. She has a shop on Swinegate," explained the young constable.

Shadow scowled and pointed an accusing finger at Jimmy. "I'll bet this is another of your smashed windows, wasting more time!"

Jimmy opened his mouth to protest, but Shadow was already stalking away down the corridor.

THE LADY WAS waiting for them in the reception area. She was tall and her ample frame was hidden beneath loose-fitting black trousers and a sort of patchwork-style tunic. Her dark hair was piled on top of her head and seemed to be secured with two diagonal chopsticks. She smiled and lifted her hand expectantly when the two detectives appeared. She was wearing silver rings on all of her fingers. Shadow gave Jimmy a meaningful look. There was no way he was going to involve himself in the shop window saga. Jimmy held out his hand and stepped forward.

"Hello, Miss Treanor, I'm Sergeant Chang. How can I help?"

"Oh, hello, Sergeant. Please call me Ellie – everyone does. Well, it is a bit of a delicate matter," she began. "You see I have a little shop on Swingate. Perhaps I should say studio. Yes, that would be more accurate."

Shadow groaned inwardly. They would be here all day.

"Is there a problem with the shop or studio?" asked Jimmy.

Miss Treanor shook her head and a few wisps of hair escaped and fell round her face. "Oh no, not at all – everything there is fine. It's just, you see, I design jewellery there. Sometimes my own designs, sometimes special commissions for customers."

Shadow's ears suddenly pricked up. He stepped forward and held out his hand.

"Chief Inspector Shadow, Miss Treanor. Would your business happen to be called Ellie Treanor Designs: ETD?"

"Yes, that's right, Chief Inspector." She beamed.

"Then please take a seat," he said, gesturing to the black plastic chairs that were secured to the wall with screws. As there were only two chairs, Jimmy was left standing. With a sigh he pulled out his electronic notebook while Shadow took over.

"Miss Treanor, is it possible you designed a bangle recently for a customer? A particularly nice piece in gold with cats' heads at either end?" Shadow was sitting opposite the lady now and giving her his full attention.

Miss Treanor opened her eyes very wide. "Why yes, Chief Inspector. How clever of you. It's known as a 'Cats of Freya' bangle and was a commission."

"For Alfred Campbell?"

"Right again, I have to say. I was dreading coming here, but you are making this so much easier. You see Mr Campbell collected the bangle a few days ago. He asked me to send the invoice to his accountant and then, well, I read about what happened and thought if he hadn't mentioned it to his accountant then…"

She trailed off, but Shadow nodded, an understanding expression on his face.

"You have concerns regarding payment of the invoice. May I ask how much it was for, Miss Treanor?"

"Six thousand pounds," replied the jewellery designer.

"Crikey, are all the pieces you design that expensive?" asked Jimmy.

Shadow closed his eyes for a second. Would his sergeant never learn?

"Not at all, Sergeant Chang," Miss Treanor said, turning to Jimmy with a smile. "It's all down to the materials I use. Had I used silver and not added the precious stones the bangle would have been much less expensive."

"And do you only design Viking jewellery?" Jimmy pressed on as Shadow continued to glower at him.

"I take my inspiration for all cultures and ages, Sergeant, or clients can bring their own designs to me," replied Miss Treanor.

"Did Mr Campbell design the bangle?" asked Shadow; he was determined to take back control of the discussion.

The lady turned to face him again. "Not exactly, Chief Inspector. He showed me an old photograph of a real Viking 'Cats of Freya' bangle that he had found many years ago, but that had been sold to a museum, and he told me he wanted a copy. Now, the photograph wasn't very good quality, so I thought I'd do my own detective work, if you'll pardon the pun, Chief Inspector." She giggled and Shadow forced himself to smile at her joke. "I looked into which museums had bought pieces from the Fulford Hoard, with the hope that I could either visit them or if they were abroad, they might send me a more up-to-date photo, but I couldn't find it anywhere. It was very strange. In the end I just had to try my best with the old picture."

"I see, Miss Treanor, and did Mr Campbell say if the bangle was to commemorate a special occasion at all?"

"He didn't say, Chief Inspector. I researched the history, as I do with every piece I design. Apparently, the goddess Freya had her chariot pulled by two cats and she is meant to symbolise love, beauty, fertility, and gold, so make of that what you will." She leant back in her chair with a self-conscious laugh and a few more strands of hair escaped. Shadow stood up and held out his hand once more.

"Thank you very much for coming to see us, Miss Treanor. Your help has been invaluable. If you could leave your business card and invoice with us, I'll make sure it's passed on to the accountants and confirm your claim is legitimate."

Miss Treanor produced an envelope from the pocket of her tunic and handed it to Shadow. "Thank you so much, Chief Inspector. You have really put my mind at rest. Thank you too, Sergeant," she called.

After she had gone, Shadow handed the envelope straight to Jimmy.

"Well, she turned out to be more useful than I was expecting. Find out who can sort that out for her, will you? Now, let's get back to Mr Bennington."

EDWARD BENNINGTON OWNED Jorvik Books, a shop on Fossgate dedicated to selling reading material with a Viking theme. It was in a tall, narrow building between a café and a hairdresser's salon. Inside it was poorly lit and had a musty slightly damp smell. Tall bookcases reaching almost to the ceiling were crammed into every available space. Shadow and Jimmy were both quite surprised to find it not only open on a Sunday, but also that several customers were browsing the heaving shelves. A very pretty blonde young woman was perched on an old oak table by the door. Shadow had heard the words *ethereal beauty* used many times, but it was not often he saw it in the flesh. She looked up from her book and smiled when the two detectives entered.

"Hello, can I help you?"

Not wanting to alarm the customers, Shadow discreetly opened his warrant card and showed it to her.

"We were hoping to speak with Mr Bennington, if possible," he said. The woman didn't show any hint of surprise at the arrival of two police officers in the shop on a Sunday.

"Of course, he's in his office. I'll show you up there."

Shadow and Jimmy followed her through what felt like a

labyrinth of tall, tightly packed bookcases, all crammed with dusty, weighty-looking tomes. She led them up a narrow, twisting flight of stairs and then another. Shadow wished she would slow down. He wasn't sure, but he thought she might be the girl he had seen with Dan and Will the night before. If only he hadn't been so out of breath, he would have asked her. Each time she climbed a step the hem of her trousers rose high enough to show some unusual markings on her ankle. Shadow wasn't the only one to notice.

"Cool tattoo," commented Jimmy. The woman smiled as she glanced down.

"Thanks, it's my name written in runes from the Viking alphabet."

"How do you find what your name is in runes?" asked Jimmy.

"Well, in my case, Edward told me, but I think there's an app you can use, not just for runes, lots of different languages too."

"Really? That sounds great, thanks!"

Shadow shook his head as he trudged after them both. His sergeant seemed to be very easily distracted these days. He also found it very strange that so many people associated with this investigation had tattoos. Personally, the thought of a stranger attacking him with a needle in the name of art filled him with horror. Finally, their blonde guide came to a stop in front of a door. She knocked briskly and called out.

"Dad, there are two policemen here to see you."

There was no reply. Jimmy and Shadow exchanged a look of surprise. Neither could believe such a striking girl could be related to the rather underwhelming Edward. She opened the door and waved them through into the office.

"Can I get either of you a tea or coffee?" she asked.

"No thanks," replied Jimmy, after looking at Shadow, who was leaning on the door frame, still trying to catch his breath. She smiled again and disappeared back down the stairs.

"Thank you, Astrid!" called out Edward, although neither detective could see him. He emerged from behind his leather-topped desk that was piled high with yet more books.

"Hello there, Chief Inspector Shadow, it's nice to see you again. Good afternoon, Sergeant Chang," he greeted them, while at the same time scurrying around clearing away papers and books from chairs, so there was enough space for them all to sit down.

"Good afternoon, Mr Bennington. The young lady who showed us up here is your daughter?" asked Shadow, who had now recovered after the climb.

"Stepdaughter," corrected Edward. "Astrid was only a baby when I married Agnetha, her mother. I'm afraid I never met her father."

Edward handed him a framed photograph of a beautiful blonde woman clearly taken some years ago. She had long flowing hair and bright blue eyes. Her likeness to Astrid was uncanny.

"Agnetha and Astrid are both unusual names," observed Shadow as he returned the photo.

"Not in Norway, Chief Inspector. I met them both when I was studying over there, in Trondheim, many moons ago now."

"And does Mrs Bennington work here with you?" Shadow enquired.

Edward's expression clouded and he shook his head. "No, Chief Inspector, I'm afraid my wife died almost twenty-five years ago, while giving birth to our son, Bjorn."

"I'm very sorry to hear that," sympathised Shadow, and Edward gave a weak smile.

"Incidentally, she was never Mrs Bennington. Agnetha was proud of her Norwegian roots, as of course she should be. She kept her name, Agnetha Andersen."

There was an awkward pause. Edward looked so sad Shadow felt almost guilty to raise the subject of yet more deaths. The silence was suddenly shattered by a loud screech. A large black bird flew down from the tall bookcase behind them and across the room. Both detectives ducked. Shadow could feel the breeze from its wings on the back of his neck as it swooped and landed on Edward's shoulder.

"For crying out loud!" Shadow exclaimed, unable to hide his shock.

"Oh, don't mind Tostig, Chief Inspector. He is quite harmless." Edward laughed, stroking the bird's beak affectionately.

"What is it – a crow?" asked Jimmy.

"No, Sergeant, he's a raven. Of course, the great god Odin had two ravens – Hugin and Munin – but I am a mere mortal. Odin also had two wolves – Geri and Freki – but I thought that might be a step too far in the centre of York." He chuckled, almost to himself.

"I understand you're quite the expert when it comes to Vikings, Mr Bennington," said Shadow, having regained his composure.

"Oh, I wouldn't say an expert, Chief Inspector – it is after all a vast subject – but I have devoted many years to studying them and their culture. They have held a certain fascination for me for, oh, as long as I can remember. I suppose it must have been growing up here in York. Even today, no matter where you look, we are surrounded by Vikings."

Jimmy glanced around and his confusion must have shown in his face. Edward smiled indulgently.

"I am, of course, speaking metaphorically, Sergeant, but if you consider for a moment how many of our street names end in gate, for example, Fossgate, Coppergate, Goodramgate to name just a few. All from the Viking *gata* meaning street. However, I recently discovered my interest in the Vikings may not merely be a coincidence.

"Astrid bought me one of those new DNA testing kits for Christmas and it turns out eighty per cent of my ancestors were from Scandinavia. Isn't that marvellous?" He beamed at the two police officers. Shadow nodded politely but looking at the slightly built man in front of him, with his watery blue eyes behind half-moon spectacles perched on his nose, he couldn't help thinking Edward's warrior ancestors might be a little disappointed in their descendent.

"If we could ask you a few questions about Alfred's death?" Shadow suggested, trying to steer the conversation back to the present day.

"Oh yes, Alfred's death," agreed Edward readily. "I've been thinking about all the connotations. Firstly, as I told you, there's Alfred's name. The Anglo-Saxon king who united the country and defeated the Vikings was killed when he played the role of Ragnar. Is that significant? Also, how apt was it that Alfred should be discovered in St George's Field, a place that was once the site of public executions."

Shadow frowned. Edward seemed to be analysing the death of Alfred as though it was an historic event, not a modern-day crime.

"Execution implies punishment for a crime committed. What crime had Alfred committed?" he asked, but before Edward could reply, there was a deep laugh behind them. They all turned their heads. Standing in the doorway was a tall well-built man in his early twenties with dark eyes and hair down to his shoulders, and a stubbly beard.

"Where do you start when it comes to Alfred Campbell and his crimes? You two flatfoots have got no chance," he sneered.

Shadow bristled. He hadn't heard that insult since his days as a young PC, out on the beat in London.

"Oh, hello, Bjorn," said Edward, who seemed flustered all of a sudden. "Chief Inspector, Sergeant Chang, this is my son, Bjorn."

The raven screeched again and flew from Edward's shoulder to the top of one of the bookcases.

"Stupid bloody bird!" snarled Bjorn, ignoring Jimmy's outstretched hand. "I need to borrow some money, Dad."

"Yes, right, of course." Edward hurried over to a safe in the corner of the room and tapped in a code. "How much would you like, Bjorn? Will a hundred be enough?"

"Make it two," came the blunt response.

The policemen both watched as Edward meekly handed over a bundle of twenty-pound notes and Bjorn quickly counted them without offering a word of thanks.

"Do you think Alfred deserved to die?" Shadow asked. Bjorn didn't bother to look at him as he folded the notes and stuffed them into his pocket.

"I think in this world, when you're successful you make enemies, that's all." With that he turned and disappeared downstairs as quickly as he had arrived, his heavy footsteps echoing after him.

Shadow thought Bjorn had ensured his arrival was far quieter than his departure.

"I'm sorry about Bjorn, Chief Inspector," apologised Edward as he retook his seat.

"Your son has a point though, Mr Bennington. Alfred treated many people badly by all accounts, including you regarding the Fulford Hoard. He used your knowledge and cheated you."

Edward gave a sigh of resignation. "That was many years ago, Chief Inspector, and it was all on his land after all. I was just happy Alfred still wanted me to be involved with the Daneholm museum and the festival."

"Were all the items found in the Fulford Hoard photographed?" Shadow enquired, thinking about the bangle.

"I believe so and catalogued, although most of that was done by the archaeologists under the supervision of the coroner's office. They had to be informed within fourteen days of any treasure found, as I am sure you know. However, Alfred was kind enough to let me choose the pieces to go in Daneholm. That gave me more pleasure than mere money and as I always say life's too short to bear a grudge."

"Really, that doesn't sound very Viking. I thought they were all about settling blood feuds," said Jimmy.

"No, no, Sergeant Chang, that's a common misconception. They were peace-loving people. That is what sometimes used to upset me about the festival. With Alfred in charge, there was too much focus on the violence and warfare. I always tried to suggest incorporating more of their artistic heritage instead of making them sound like bloodthirsty warriors."

Edward stood up and moved his chair closer to the

bookcase. He climbed on top and began attempting to coax down the raven.

"I thought that's exactly what they were?" queried Jimmy. "All that raiding and pillaging."

"Oh no, Sergeant, they were great storytellers and poets too. People are always amazed when I tell them how much they have influenced our own culture. For example, 'The Curse of Andvari's Ring' was a huge inspiration to Tolkien."

"Who?" mouthed Jimmy as Edward faced the other way.

"*Lord of the Rings*," mouthed back Shadow, a second before Edward looked round.

"And I am sure I do not need to tell you, Chief Inspector, which great play was inspired by the legend of Amleth, the Prince of Denmark. My goodness, it's even an anagram."

Jimmy, even more puzzled, turned again to Shadow.

The chief inspector despaired. His deputy's knowledge of literature was worse than his grasp of history. "*Hamlet* by Shakespeare," he hissed as the raven finally jumped down on to Edward's outstretched arm.

"And there are many more tales I can tell you about…"

AGAIN, IT WAS growing dark when the two detectives finally emerged from the bookshop.

"Well, that's an hour of my life I won't get back again," grumbled Shadow as he turned up the collar of his jacket against the cool evening air.

"I even gave up taking notes," agreed Jimmy, rubbing his hand wearily across his eyes. "What do you think, Chief? Any chance Edward could be our killer?"

"Possibly, but he wouldn't have needed that sword though. He could have just bored them both to death."

"What about Bjorn? You wouldn't want to bump into him on a dark night, would you?"

"No, he was certainly overlooked when they were handing out charm. Tomorrow check and see if he's got form – I'll be surprised if he hasn't. By the way, where did you say Chloe's bag was found?"

Jimmy pointed down Fossgate to the bridge over the Foss, the smaller of the two rivers that flowed through the city.

"Just down the road, Chief. The fisherman said it was caught up in weeds near the Merchant Adventurers' Hall."

Shadow turned back to the shop. Astrid had appeared again. She was busy putting some books back on the shelves.

"You get off home, Sergeant. I think I'll nip back in for a moment," he said.

"You must be a glutton for punishment, Chief," said Jimmy, shaking his head as he turned and walked back up the road.

Shadow thought he may well be right but headed back into the shop anyway. Astrid looked surprised to see him.

"Did you forget something, Chief Inspector?"

"No, but talking to your father was so interesting, I was wondering if you had a book about Viking legends?"

Astrid gave him a wry smile but walked over to one of the bookcases and ran her finger along the row of books, before picking one out and handing it to Shadow. It was a hard-back edition of *Vikings – Their Greatest Myths and Legends*, and he noticed the foreword was written by E Bennington.

"That looks perfect, thank you." He smiled. "It must be nice to work with your father. Are you here every day?"

Astrid shook her head as she handed him a bag for the book and noted the sale down in a large ledger. There didn't appear to be a conventional till, only a metal cash box and drawer in the old oak table for notes.

"No, I just help out on Sundays, so Dad can catch up with his paperwork. At least that's what he's supposed to be doing, but I usually end up doing his VAT receipts and accounts at the end of each month anyway. As you can no doubt see, Dad isn't exactly the most clued-up businessman."

"So where do you usually work?"

"I'm a solicitor at Rutherfords'."

Shadow was surprised. Rutherfords' was one of the most well-respected legal practices in the city and he thought he knew most of the solicitors who worked there.

"Really, I don't recall our paths having crossed before?"

"I specialise in family law." Astrid smiled. "So unless something has gone horribly wrong with a divorce, there's not much call for me to interact with CID, Chief Inspector."

Shadow smiled too and decided to try to change the subject. "We met your brother, Bjorn, while we were upstairs," he began.

"He's not my brother," she corrected him immediately and her smile swiftly disappeared.

"Sorry, half-brother," apologised Shadow quickly.

"I assume he was scrounging as usual. Did he make Dad give him some money?" Astrid asked testily.

"Yes. Two hundred pounds."

Astrid's eyes flashed angrily, and she gave a shake of her head.

"Some things never change. Dad will bankrupt himself rather than say no to him and Bjorn knows it."

"Some fathers are like that. They'll do anything for their children," Shadow suggested as Astrid continued to frown. "By the way, did you know Alfred Campbell?" he ventured.

"Not really," she replied.

"I only ask because I thought I saw you last night with Dan and Will Campbell."

"Yes, you probably did," she agreed. "We grew up together, but their dad was never really around."

"What about Chloe? Did you know her?"

"I met her briefly, once or twice," she said evenly. "I acted for Dan during their annulment."

"Really?" asked Shadow, slightly surprised. This was a connection he had not anticipated. "And how did their annulment go?"

Astrid's face broke into a broad smile once more. "The whole thing was a total farce," she declared, "and just so you know, Chief Inspector, you could have asked me all these questions without having to buy a book. Happy reading!"

She gave him a knowing wink as she handed over his change and Shadow was aware he had been dismissed.

CHAPTER SIX

Down 3 (6 letters)
A solicitor? At Yale we find many studying

A S SHADOW LEFT the bookshop, he decided to walk home via the Merchant Adventurers' Hall. The entranceway was through a narrow passage, almost hidden about halfway down Fossgate. Most people who didn't know of its existence walked right past it.

The hall was one of several surviving medieval buildings erected by the various city guilds. As the name suggested, it had been built in the 1300s by merchants who used the river to trade. It was a beautiful half-timbered building that was now hired out for private functions. Surrounded by pretty gardens that led down to the Foss, it was an oasis of calm hidden away in the bustling city.

Shadow wandered down to the river. He saw the reeds where Chloe's bag must have been found and paused to watch a pair of ducks glide by. It was such a tranquil scene that it was difficult to imagine the river had ever been busy with boats trading goods, never mind full of longboats arriving with invading Vikings. Shadow left the garden by the steps that led up to Piccadilly and, happily, realised he was right on time for Gepetto's opening their doors.

AFTER AN EARLY supper of spaghetti carbonara, Shadow returned to *Florence*. It was a chilly night. A cool wind whistled down the Ouse, rattling the windows of the boat. Shadow settled in front of his log burner with Ella Fitzgerald playing in the background and a glass of Valpolicella in his hand. The book about Vikings lay open on his knee.

He had read about the legend of Ragnar and his sons, the story Edward was telling at the festival, and now he was flicking through it casually. He stopped to read the odd page here and there, but his thoughts kept drifting back to the case. So much of it made no sense. The blindfold was bothering him – like an itch he could not scratch. It seemed likely that Alfred had put it on himself, but why? He remembered what Edward had said about St George's Field being a place for public executions. Didn't the condemned man wear a blindfold before he was hanged or beheaded?

His eyes suddenly focused on the page with the word *Haustblot*. That was the name of the Heathen celebration the York Viking Festival was designed to coincide with. He read the description. It was a ceremony to give thanks for the harvest at the time of the autumn equinox. The *blot* part of the word referred to the ritual sacrifices made to the gods during the ceremony, usually animal, but sometimes human. Shadow frowned. Was somebody making sure the Vikings still influenced what happened in York today?

THAT NIGHT SHADOW dreamt of a battle between two Viking armies. As the swords and axes of the warriors clashed, above them flew three winged Valkyries, deciding who below would live or die. When they turned to show their faces, they were revealed to be Annabel, Astrid and Chloe.

He woke with a start and shivered. He was freezing cold. Bleary-eyed he looked round. His duvet was lying in a heap on the floor. He must have kicked it off while he was dreaming. At that moment, his alarm clock began to ring. With a groan he stretched out an arm to silence it and reached for his dressing gown. His mood was not improved when he remembered that Bettys would not open until mid-morning due to maintenance work.

He went into the galley, made a pot of tea, and managed to find a packet of digestive biscuits that were only a week out of date and still had a slight crunch. Then he telephoned Jimmy.

"Chief? Is that you? What's wrong?"

Shadow frowned in irritation. Just because he didn't walk round with his phone permanently attached to his ear like some didn't mean there was always a drama unfolding when he did choose to use it.

"Nothing's wrong, but when you get Chloe's keys back from forensics come and meet me outside the Old Bonding Warehouse. I'm not going to walk all the way to the station only to come back here again."

With that he hung up. One hour and a whole packet of biscuits later, Shadow was showered and dressed and in a slightly improved mood. The morning sun was bright, but the air was chilly as he stepped on to the towpath. The red and gold leaves that had been clinging to the trees now created a carpet that crunched beneath his feet. As he looked across the river, he could see Ragnar's Palace and the rest of the Viking encampment being dismantled. He wondered if it would return next year. The Old Bonding Warehouse was on Skeldergate just a short walk along the path going under the bridge that shared its name.

Shadow could remember when he was a child, the warehouse had still been used to store goods unloaded from barges coming into the city. From the outside, the original white walkways and caging for the cranes and pulleys were still visible. Then times changed and it had stood empty and unused for several years until Alfred Campbell had bought it and turned it into apartments.

Jimmy was waiting for him outside the warehouse. For once he wasn't on his phone. Instead his arms were wrapped around his body and he was stamping his feet. Shadow knew his deputy was not a fan of cold weather.

"Winter's on its way, perhaps you should invest in a scarf and gloves instead of those expensive trainers, Sergeant," Shadow suggested unsympathetically.

There were only three keys on the red stiletto keyring. The first one Jimmy tried let them into the entrance lobby.

"By the way, Chief," said Jimmy as they waited for the lift, "I sorted payment for the bracelet out with the accountants and went to tell Miss Treanor. She was really pleased. Then I checked up on the Benningtons this morning. Astrid and Bjorn both still live at home with Edward, in Fulford like the Campbells. You were right, Bjorn has got form. A few years ago, he got a six-month sentence for common assault. He had a job as a bouncer, working at Valhalla."

"Alfred's Viking nightclub?" interrupted Shadow.

Jimmy nodded. "That's right. He got into an argument with a customer one night, went a bit too far, and broke his nose. He was convicted and lost his job."

"It must have been difficult for him to get work again after that," reasoned Shadow.

"That's probably why he set up his own security business. AAB Security. It sounds impressive when you read its adverts, but it's really just Bjorn and a few casual employees."

"But that's the company that provided security for the Viking Festival," said Shadow in surprise. "Why would Alfred give the contract to such a small company and someone he'd already sacked once?"

"Maybe he felt sorry for him," suggested Jimmy with a shrug, then winced.

"Are you all right?"

"Yes, Chief, only a cramp," said Jimmy as they stepped through the lift's sliding door.

"AAB," repeated Shadow, half to himself while they glided up to the top floor of the building.

WHEN THEY ARRIVED, they used the two remaining keys to open the door into the duplex. They walked through into a vast space that still retained much of the building's industrial heritage. The walls were all exposed red brick, and the original metal girders and pipes still jutted out here and there. Two huge arched windows gave an incredible view of the city, looking across the river to Clifford's Tower and, in the distance, the Minster.

The furnishings, however, were very modern. Several massive leather sofas were arranged around the room and a vast television screen was hung on one wall. There was a cocktail bar in one corner complete with a pink neon sign and along another wall were several tall fridges packed with champagne. There was even room for a full-sized snooker table. Jimmy gave a low whistle.

"Wow, Alfred certainly knew how to have a good time, didn't he, Chief."

Shadow did not respond. He was more interested in what was not there. Apart from one faded polaroid of Dan as a little boy in a Viking costume stuck to the mirror behind the bar, there were no photographs of Alfred's family anywhere to be seen.

Shadow climbed the spiral wrought-iron staircase up to the next level. He pushed open what he guessed was the door to the bedroom. It was another vast room dominated by a bed that must have been at least nine feet wide. The bed was covered with leopard-print cushions that Shadow assumed were Chloe's influence. There were also plenty of framed photos of Chloe and Alfred grinning with their arms draped around each other, despite them only being together for a few months.

Shadow left the bedroom and entered what appeared to be Alfred's office. There were several large leather swivel chairs and a glass-top table holding a computer, printer, and laptop. A metal filing cabinet in the corner of the room caught his eye. It was the type that could be locked, but there was a noticeable dent on the top of the outer frame and the upper drawer was slightly open. It had been broken into. He found a pen in one of his pockets and being careful his fingers did not touch the cabinet, he eased the drawer open.

Drop-down folders containing various documents hung inside. Again, using the top of the pen, Shadow flicked through them. The folder labelled "bank statements" was empty. He called out to Jimmy.

"What's up, Chief?" asked Jimmy as he clattered up the stairs and arrived in the office.

"Somebody got here before us," said Shadow, showing the sergeant the empty folder. "Call forensics and get them to come and check for prints. Also check if Alfred's keys have turned up anywhere."

Jimmy immediately began tapping on his phone as Shadow headed to the door.

"Where are you going, Chief?"

"I think it's time I paid Martin Plunkett a visit."

"The solicitor?"

"Yes," replied Shadow, pointing to a photo of Alfred and Martin sitting together on a yacht in the sunshine somewhere. "How many people do you know who have a photo of their solicitor on their desk?"

MARTIN PLUNKETT'S OFFICES were in a large, modern, purpose-built block on Peasholme Green. They were impossible to miss, as the name Plunkett's was emblazoned across it in large gold letters. Shadow thought all the glass and shiny letters looked terribly out of place standing next to the medieval city walls. However, he also thought such a large and striking building must mean business was going very well for Martin Plunkett.

In the car park there was a large gold Mercedes with the

personalised number plate MMP 7. Shadow had met Martin Plunkett briefly once or twice. Unfortunately, he was rather good at keeping his clients out of prison. He was also a well-recognised figure around the city. As well as having a prominent law firm, he had also served for many years as a city councillor.

The solicitor's attractive, well-groomed secretary gave Shadow a look of disdain as he stood in front of her desk.

"I'm here to see Martin Plunkett," he said pleasantly.

"Mr Plunkett is far too busy to see anyone without an appointment," she replied, haughtily turning back to her computer screen. Shadow sighed as he removed his warrant card from his pocket. He never enjoyed being heavy-handed. He placed his identification on the desk.

"I'm afraid I was informing, not requesting, miss."

The secretary suddenly lost her composure when she saw the warrant card and hurried away through the door behind her. A few seconds later the office door opened and out stepped Martin Plunkett. He greeted Shadow with a dazzling smile and a firm handshake.

"Chief Inspector Shadow! How wonderful to see you! What a pleasure!" he enthused.

Shadow raised a sceptical eyebrow as he followed the solicitor into his office and sat down. His welcome was over the top to say the least. Nobody ever thought the arrival of a senior police officer at their place of work was "wonderful". They were invariably the bearers of bad news in some shape or form. In fact, as Shadow sat opposite Martin Plunkett and studied him, he realised it wasn't only his words that were false. Everything about the man looked artificial. From his glowing tan and glossy chestnut hair without a trace of grey to his gleaming straight white teeth. No Englishman had teeth like that; it was unnatural.

"Can Amanda get you a tea or coffee? Something stronger maybe?" Plunkett asked, gesturing towards an impressive collection of single malts arranged on a glass shelf next to photographs of himself with various local dignitaries. Shadow spotted the chief constable and the lord mayor amongst them.

"No, thank you," Shadow said, nodding at the pouting secretary who was waiting in the doorway. She disappeared, closing the door behind her with a loud click.

"I can only assume you are here about poor old Alfred, Chief Inspector," began Plunkett, taking his seat behind the desk.

"Yes, I understand he was a client of yours."

"That's right. Here at Plunkett's we handled all his legal work, but he was so much more than merely a client. Alf was a friend of mine, a mate."

"Then I'm sorry for your loss. I'm afraid I haven't come across many who would say the same, Mr Plunkett."

The solicitor threw his head back and laughed as if Shadow had just told the most hilarious joke. "Ha ha, Chief Inspector, you may have a point there, but I always thought of Alf as a lovable rogue. No saint certainly, but then there are always those who begrudged him his good fortune. Jealousy can be a terrible thing, Chief Inspector."

"Indeed, it can, Mr Plunkett. Now, when you say you handled all Mr Campbell's legal work, does that mean personal as well as business?"

"It certainly does." He suddenly leaned forward across the desk and whispered, conspiratorially, "Do you want to know what's in the will?"

Shadow was a little taken aback but before he could reply, Martin leaned back in his chair, opened his arms theatrically, and announced, "Dan gets it all! Everything! Lock, stock, and barrel! Which, considering the two of them barely spoke these days, is quite something."

"What about Will?" asked Shadow. Martin looked at him as if he were mad.

"Will? Will gets nothing." Martin leaned forward again and, tapping the side of his forehead with his index finger, he whispered, "You know he's not all there, Chief Inspector. Alfred always thought he should be put in a home – you know with people to take care of him, for his own good."

Out of sight, out of mind more like, thought Shadow.

"Is this common knowledge? The will, I mean, and Mr Campbell's feelings towards his younger son?"

"Well, I don't think any of it was a secret."

"Were you also involved with Mr Campbell's divorce from Annabel?"

"Oh, Alfred played a blinder there." Plunkett grinned. "It could have cost him an absolute fortune, but he got away with paying her a pittance."

"Didn't Annabel want any money?"

"Not really. All she cared about was staying in the family home and having full custody of the little boys, as they were then."

"Who acted for Mrs Campbell?"

"Rutherford, the old fossil! I thought he would have fought harder to protect her interests. Although, funnily enough, they did request a meeting with Alfred a couple of weeks ago. Maybe he wanted to renegotiate. Better late than never, eh?"

Martin laughed loudly again at his own joke.

"And the marriage between Dan and Chloe? Were you also negotiating the legal end to that relationship?"

"Actually, we managed to get that one annulled."

"Really? I understood annulling a marriage was quite difficult these days."

"It can be, but then luckily Chloe made a statement saying she had been forced into the marriage."

"Was that true?"

"Dan didn't dispute her claim. I find there's always a way around these things, Chief Inspector, if you know what I mean." He tapped the side of his nose and winked.

Shadow did not know what he meant and right now he wasn't sure he wanted to. No wonder Astrid had referred to the annulment as "a farce".

"Just one more thing, Mr Plunkett. As far as you were aware, were Alfred and Chloe planning on getting married?"

The bangle was bothering Shadow. Was it simply a gift or could it signify something more?

Martin began chuckling again. "I doubt it. Chloe was a pretty, fun-loving girl, but Alfred liked to play the field. Don't we all given half a chance, Chief Inspector." He gave another loud guffaw.

Shadow stood up to leave. He had heard enough. "Thank you for your help, Mr Plunkett."

"Any time at all, Chief Inspector. My door is always open." The solicitor clasped both his hands round Shadow's outstretched one. Shadow could not help but notice his heavy gold watch and the three gold rings he wore.

"That reminds me," he said, "before I came here, I visited Mr Campbell's home. I am sorry to inform you that we believe there has been a burglary. Some items have been stolen. Our forensics team are there at the moment and as you are handling Mr Campbell's estate, I will make sure you are kept informed of any developments."

"Thank you, Chief Inspector," replied Plunkett with a little less enthusiasm and his megawatt smile dimming ever so slightly.

SHADOW GAVE A small shudder as he walked away from Plunkett's office. Something about the meeting had left him feeling quite grubby. Well, grubby and hungry. Fortunately, standing on the other side of Peasholme Green was the Black Swan. The Mucky Duck, as it was affectionately known, was a timber-framed building with leaded light windows. It was one of the city's oldest pubs. The plaque by the door told visitors it had first been built in 1417.

Shadow stepped inside, ducking his head so he didn't hit the low wooden beams. He went to the bar and ordered a pint of Theakston's Old Peculier and a giant Yorkshire pudding filled with roast beef, mashed potato, vegetables, and gravy. Then he found a high-backed settle facing the open fire, sat down and opened his *Yorkshire Post*. Half an hour later his crossword was complete, and a waitress was clearing away his empty plate. Feeling more content than he had all day, Shadow stretched his legs out towards the fire, listened to the hypnotic crackling of the logs, and contemplated the case.

The more he learnt about Alfred Campbell, the less he liked him. The man had clearly been a bully, a very wealthy bully, but still a bully. Like most wealthy bullies, he thought his money gave him a licence to behave badly, whilst surrounding himself with sycophants who encouraged him. In Alfred's case, recently this seemed to be Chloe and Martin Plunkett.

It reminded Shadow of when he had been at boarding

school. The bully there was called Cartwright – Philip Cartwright and his two sidekicks, Hughes and Jones. Cartwright was tall, good at sport, and from a well-off family, yet he still felt the need to pick on those who were different or weaker than him. Shadow had been an easy target with his scholarship and northern accent. Fortunately, he had been able to stand up for himself, but there were other weaker boys whose lives Cartwright and his cronies had made hell.

Shadow's thoughts were suddenly interrupted by the harsh sound of a chair leg loudly scraping across the floor behind him and an angry voice saying, "I want nothing more to do with you. Don't ever contact me again!"

Shadow knew that voice. He had heard it less than an hour ago. It was Martin Plunkett. Sure enough, just then the solicitor strode quickly by, outside the window, back towards his office. Shadow cursed himself for not paying more attention to the other patrons. He hadn't even noticed Plunkett was there.

Carefully, Shadow turned his head to one side, pressing his eye up against the back of the settle. The old wood had contracted over the centuries and there was a long crack running down the middle. It was only about a quarter of an inch, but wide enough to peer through. He looked one way and then the other until he spotted who Martin must have been speaking to.

Sitting at the table right behind him, scowling into his whisky, was Bjorn Bennington. There was a muscle twitching in his cheek and his knuckles were white as they gripped the glass. Shadow stood up, edged his way round the settle, and approached the younger man's table.

"Hello, Bjorn," he said evenly. "Do you mind if I join you?"

Bjorn looked up and scowled. "I don't drink with coppers," he snarled, but Shadow was not easily put off.

"It was a nice gesture calling your company AAB Security, after your mother. Her initials were AAB were they not? Agnetha Andersen Bennington."

Bjorn looked at Shadow as if he was an utter fool. "It's AAB because it means it's always first in the phone book. It's nothing to do with my stupid mother," he snapped and all at once, he threw back the last of his drink, pushed his chair back, and stomped out of the pub.

Shadow quickly pulled on his wax jacket and followed Bjorn outside. The angry young man was heading down towards Stonebow, roughly pushing past anyone who got in his way. There goes another bully, he thought. One who even picks on his own father. Suddenly Bjorn stopped and turned into the Terrace, a sports bar full of television screens that boldly advertised all the premiership matches you could watch inside.

Shadow was considering following him when the mobile phone in his coat pocket began to buzz. It was always turned to silent and he left it inside his coat that had been folded on the seat opposite him in the pub. He took it out and looked at the screen. There were several missed calls and messages from Jimmy. Shadow shook his head. Bjorn would have to wait for now.

HE ARRIVED BACK at the Old Bonding Warehouse and Jimmy buzzed him in. When he entered the duplex, he was surprised to find Sophie sitting in one of the swivel chairs in Alfred's office, opposite Jimmy, who was intently tapping away on the laptop.

"What are you doing here?" he asked, sounding less friendly than he had meant to.

"Nice to see you too, Chief." She grinned. "I'm just dropping off a sandwich and a coffee for Jimmy. We were due to meet for lunch, but he got engrossed here and I also wanted to check on his arm."

"What's wrong with his arm?" asked Shadow as Jimmy quickly looked up and began shaking his head furiously at Sophie, who burst out laughing.

"Haven't you told him?" She giggled.

"Obviously not," groaned Jimmy as he raked his hand through his floppy fringe in despair.

Shadow looked at the two of them, completely confused. "What is going on?"

With a sigh, Jimmy slowly shrugged off his leather jacket and cautiously rolled up his sleeve to reveal a white dressing.

"I got a tattoo last night, Chief," he explained, lifting the edge of the dressing to show Shadow a patch of angry red skin around a line of black markings. "It's my dad's name in Chinese. All these people we kept meeting with Viking tattoos made me want to do something to celebrate my own heritage."

"I see," replied Shadow, taking the briefest of looks at Jimmy's arm. He grimaced then quickly stepped back and turned to Sophie.

"Please tell me you didn't get one as well?"

"No way!" Sophie smiled with a shake of her head. "I saw far too many skin infections when I was a junior doctor. Nobody is coming near me with a needle without a good medical reason."

"Well, thanks heavens for that. Where are forensics anyway. Not late again?" he asked.

"Been and gone, Chief," replied Jimmy as he carefully rolled his sleeve back down.

"Did they find any prints on the filing cabinet?"

"No, but…"

"I don't know why we bother calling them sometimes," Shadow interrupted impatiently.

"But they did find something on one of those big drinks fridges," Jimmy continued, pointing downwards with his finger to the lower level where the champagne-packed fridges stood. "You have to use an electronic code on the keypad to open it and Sophie noticed scratch marks on the edge like from the crowbar on the filing cabinet. Forensics had a look and got a perfect thumbprint."

"Well done, Sophie," said Shadow as Sophie gave a silent bow. "Anyone we know?" he continued.

"Bjorn Bennington," replied Jimmy.

"Is that so? Well, I have just seen him having what you might call a heated conversation in the Mucky Duck with Martin Plunkett. Get on to uniform, tell them I want him brought in for questioning. He was in the Terrace when I last saw him."

"No problem, Chief, but speaking of Mr Plunkett, there's something I need to tell you first. I've managed to access electronic copies of Alfred Campbell's bank statements, all the ones that must have been stolen."

"How did you do that?"

"I hacked into Alfred's laptop. I thought it was worth a try while I was waiting for forensics. It was password-protected, but most people keep their passwords written down somewhere, I looked for an obvious place and there it was behind the photo."

Jimmy pointed to the picture of Martin and Alfred on the yacht that was now lying on the desk out of its frame.

"Good to see you haven't been wasting your time," said Shadow, quietly impressed with his sergeant. Jimmy sighed and glanced over to Sophie, who rolled her eyes. Giving compliments was not Shadow's strong point.

Shadow picked up the photo. Out of the frame the name

of the yacht was now visible. He peered at it more closely, but even without his glasses on, there was no doubt. The boat was called *Agnetha*. He turned it towards Jimmy and Sophie.

"What do you make of that?" he asked.

"Crikey, Chief!" exclaimed Jimmy.

"Who's Agnetha?" asked Sophie, looking puzzled.

"Edward Bennington's late wife. She died about twenty-five years ago," explained Jimmy.

"Have you still got the photos you took when we found Alfred's body?" asked Shadow as a thought occurred to him.

"Yes, Chief," said Jimmy, picking up his phone and scrolling through the images.

"Is there one of his tattoo?" Shadow pressed as Jimmy frowned at the screen.

"Yes, but sorry, Chief, the picture is too blurred. I think Donaldson nudged me when I was taking it."

Shadow tapped his fingers on the desk in irritation. From what he could remember the markings on Alfred's body were similar to Astrid's tattoo.

"Ask forensics if they have a photo – surely they took some."

Jimmy went back to his phone and Shadow turned to the doctor.

"Sophie, can you get your hands on the coroner's report on the death of Agnetha Andersen, possibly Agnetha Bennington. As Jimmy said, she died giving birth about twenty-five years ago. There will have been an inquest. If you could have a read-through and let me know if anything seems strange or suspicious? I'd appreciate a doctor's opinion."

"No problem, Chief," said Sophie. Not for the first time, Shadow thanked his lucky stars that Sophie was there, and he rarely had to ask Donaldson for a favour. As they were talking, Jimmy was also chatting and from the sound of things and the shaking of his head, he was not going to deliver good news. He hung up.

"Sorry, Chief, no luck."

Shadow tutted irritably. Not for the first time he wondered what the forensics team were thinking of when they attended a crime scene.

HE LEFT JIMMY and Sophie at the Old Bonding Warehouse and trudged towards the city mortuary with a heavy heart. It was a depressing place to visit at the best of times, with the lingering smell of formaldehyde and clinical white walls and floor. Today it was even worse. He was going to have to ask for that favour from Donaldson after all. When he arrived at Donaldson's office, he knocked on the door and waited, inwardly cringing. Donaldson's secretary was far more terrifying than any dragon in the Viking myths he had read last night and ferociously guarded access to her boss.

"Enter!" commanded a shrill voice from the other side.

Shadow took a deep breath and pushed the door open.

"Good afternoon," he began politely.

The secretary, with her grey hair in a tight bun and lips set in a thin line, raised an eyebrow when she saw Shadow.

"Mr Donaldson is exceedingly busy, Chief Inspector. He's due to fly out to the Algarve tomorrow. He's isn't available."

"I only need a moment of his time."

"As I said, Mr Donaldson does not have a spare moment."

"Oh, let him through, let him through, Miss Habbershaw, or we won't have a second's peace," boomed Donaldson's voice from the next room. Reluctantly, the dragon left her desk and, with a look of disapproval, showed Shadow through to Donaldson's office.

"I need to see Alfred Campbell's body again," said Shadow bluntly. He did not think it was worth wasting his breath on the usual pleasantries. Equally, Donaldson did not bother to look up from his paperwork.

"No, you don't. I presented you with an extremely thorough report."

"It didn't mention his tattoo."

"Why would it? A twenty-five-year-old inking on the skin in no way contributed to the victim's death."

Shadow held his tongue. There was no point trying to argue that, in his opinion, this was exactly the sort of thing that should be included in a report for a murder investigation.

"Did you happen to take any photographs of it?"

"No. I thought your eager young assistant took care of that. I seem to recall him getting in the way even more than usual."

Shadow didn't rise to the bait.

"Then I really do need to see the body again."

"And as I said there is no need. I can tell you the tattoo was the name *Agnetha* written in runic letters."

"Are you sure?" Shadow asked automatically, then mentally kicked himself as the doctor finally raised his head and gave the chief inspector a withering look.

"It was hardly a huge surprise."

"So, the two of them definitely had a relationship? Did many people know? Did her husband?"

Donaldson returned to whatever it was he was writing. "I'm a doctor, not a fishwife trading in gossip. You are a detective. I suggest you detect."

Shadow gave up. He had found out what he wanted to know. He turned to leave, but as he got to the door he stopped.

"By the way, I wouldn't go to Portugal just yet if I were you. The investigation is progressing quickly. When I make an arrest, you will be needed in court to give evidence to the magistrates. I'll make sure to call you as a witness."

He hurried past the dragon before he could hear Donaldson's reply. As he stepped out and deeply inhaled the fresh air, Shadow wished he felt as confident about the case as he had just sounded. If anything, it was becoming more complicated.

Edward Bennington now had two motives for wanting Alfred dead. He had been cheated out of the treasure and the love of the beautiful Agnetha. Yet, Shadow still struggled to imagine the bookish Edward as a killer. Could he have enlisted help? Perhaps his son, who he now knew had a history of violence? Then again, would Bjorn help anyone, even his father, if there wasn't something in it for him? Money perhaps? And where did Plunkett fit into it all?

THE ONLY WAY Shadow could think of to cheer himself up was to head Francesco's place on Petergate. He had missed out on his usual supper there on Friday. The restaurant was in what used to be an independent all-girls school and was another of Shadow's regular haunts. Francesco and his wife, Lucia, greeted him like a long-lost friend and showed him to his usual window seat. He knew the menu so well he didn't need to look at it before he ordered the calamari followed by the linguine allo scoglio and a bottle of Grillo.

"Everything was okay for you, Mr Shadow?" asked Lucia when she came to clear away the empty plate that a few minutes earlier had been piled high with pasta.

"Wonderful, thank you, Lucia, but I think I might have

overindulged," admitted Shadow, leaning back heavily in his chair with a satisfied sigh.

"No!" she exclaimed, patting him sympathetically on his shoulder. "You are a very busy man. You need to eat to stay strong. You must have all your strength to catch who killed Alfred and Chloe."

Shadow looked up. He was surprised to hear Lucia use their first names.

"Did you know them well, Lucia?"

Lucia shrugged. "They came here sometimes. They were good customers. He always ordered the filetto and champagne but..." she paused, raised her eyes upwards, and quickly made the sign of the cross "...he was not a nice man."

"Alfred?"

Lucia nodded and pursed her lips. "He would..." she stopped and, looking a little self-conscious, turned slightly and mimed smacking her ample behind "...to our waitresses. They are only young girls trying to do their job. They didn't like it."

"I bet they didn't. What did Chloe do when he behaved that way?"

"She encouraged him. She was a silly girl. In here they behaved like teenagers. Always giggling and..." She put down the dishes again, picked up a folded white napkin, and held it over her eyes. "He would be like this and she would feed him."

"Like a blindfold?" asked Shadow.

Lucia tutted as she shook her head disapprovingly. "Yes, Mr Shadow. It wasn't right. To behave like that in public," she continued, tutting and shaking her head as she carried the plates back to the kitchen.

Shadow took a sip of his wine. Was that why Alfred was wearing his blindfold? Was Chloe in Ragnar's Palace with him before he was killed? He recalled the two untouched glasses of wine. Had they planned an intimate supper for two? Then where was the food? Shadow groaned inwardly and topped up his glass again. So far, this case seemed to be raising far more questions than answers.

CHAPTER SEVEN

Down 4 (7 letters)
His fraudulent behaviour makes him a top cur, really

THE NEXT MORNING, Shadow was halfway through his breakfast and progressing well with his crossword when a familiar figure slipped into the chair opposite him.

"Good morning, Chief," said Sophie brightly.

"Did Jimmy put you up to this?" demanded Shadow. She'd interrupted him just when he thought he'd got nine across. "This is twice in one week my breakfast's been disturbed. It's nothing short of a conspiracy!" he continued to grumble as Julie suddenly appeared.

"Is everything all right, John?" she asked, giving Sophie a sidelong glance.

"Fine, thank you," replied Shadow, still frowning.

"Can I get your…" she paused very slightly "…friend anything?"

"No, she's not staying," said Shadow briskly.

"I only popped in to say hello," added Sophie. Julie gave her a tight smile as she slowly made her way back to the kitchens, occasionally glancing back.

"Actually, Chief, I came to tell you about the inquest into Agnetha's death, but I didn't think you'd want that broadcasting."

"Very considerate," muttered Shadow, spearing a piece of sausage with his fork. "Couldn't it have waited?"

"Nope, I'm afraid not. I'm attending a conference out at the uni all day. So, back to the inquest. Firstly, I had to sign a register at the city archive to look at it and I happened to notice, a few lines higher, the name Astrid Bennington. She must have wanted to look at the report about her mother too. That's interesting, isn't it?"

Shadow nodded begrudgingly.

"Anyway, I read the report. It was all a bit sketchy. Not as many witness statements or the medical records as I would have expected, but then it was twenty-five years ago."

"Yes, things were different then. We'd only just stopped using candles and quill pens."

"Very funny, Chief. Fortunately, the post-mortem was included, and it looks like natural causes. Agnetha was eight months pregnant. She had a fall that led to a rupture in the lining of her uterus and a massive haemorrhage…"

"Sophie, please!" objected Shadow, placing his knife and fork on the side of the plate and leaning back in his chair as a wave of nausea swept over him.

"Sorry, Chief." Sophie smiled, not looking remotely apologetic. "Anyway, it was natural causes, but it also mentioned traces of whisky in her mouth and a fairly high blood alcohol count. It sounds like she was tipsy and took a fall. They managed to save the baby, but not Agnetha. The signature on the post-mortem was Prentice's." Shadow nodded. Prentice had been the head pathologist prior to Donaldson. "But," continued Sophie, who looked like she was leading up to something, "the coroner's signature was Martin Plunkett – the solicitor you went to see yesterday. Now that has got to be more than a coincidence, Chief."

"Yes, that is interesting," admitted Shadow. He didn't know Plunkett had worked as the coroner. "Thanks, Sophie," he finally added as an image of Plunkett standing next to his single malts popped into his head.

"That's okay, I'd no idea police work was such fun," she said, grinning at Shadow's frowning face.

She pushed her chair back and Shadow was about to try to return to his cooling breakfast when a thought occurred to him. "Has Jimmy ever told you what happened to his father?"

"Yes, don't you know? It was quite a big story at the time."

Shadow shook his head. "It must have been when I was down in London."

"Well, Jimmy's parents had just moved here and opened the restaurant. One morning, his father was carrying the previous night's takings to the bank. On his way out of the bank, he saw an old lady being mugged. He chased after the guy who had stolen her handbag and managed to tackle him to the ground, but he had a knife. He slashed Jimmy's dad's throat, hit an artery." Shadow winced. "And he was dead in seconds," concluded Sophie.

"Poor Jimmy," murmured Shadow, thinking of Rose and Angela, Jimmy's mother and sister, too.

Sophie stood up and looked pointedly at Shadow's plate of bacon, sausage, and egg. "You do know animal fat is really high in cholesterol, don't you?"

"Yes, thank you, Sophie."

"I'm only thinking of your arteries! Enjoy you breakfast, Chief!"

With that she turned and breezed back through the restaurant. Shadow pushed his plate away. She had completely ruined his appetite.

WHEN SHADOW ARRIVED at the station, he found Jimmy in the incident room. He was slumped in front of a computer screen, looking very bleary-eyed.

"Have you been here all night?" asked Shadow.

"Almost," replied Jimmy with a yawn. "I couldn't sleep for thinking about the case, so I came back here and once I started digging into Alfred's finances it was difficult to stop."

"And has all this digging unearthed anything interesting?"

Shadow removed his jacket and pulled up a chair next to

his sergeant.

"It certainly has, Chief. Okay, first of all, Alfred was making fairly regular payments to a company based in Guernsey."

Guernsey was one of the Channel Islands. Also including Jersey, Alderney, and Sark, the Channel Islands were a group of small islands in the English Channel. Although crown dependencies, they were geographically closer to France. They were also offshore banking centres with very favourable tax laws.

"Annabel said Alfred had a place down there," recalled Shadow.

"Yes," agreed Jimmy as he rifled through one of the many piles of paper surrounding him, before locating the sheet he was looking for. "He owned an apartment in the capital, St Peter Port, and had a permanent berth in the marina there. Looking at his credit card payments, he sometimes flew over there from Leeds Bradford Airport, but more often he went down there in the *Agnetha*, which is currently moored in the harbour at Scarborough. Now the really interesting bit is that Alfred is one director of the Guernsey company and the other director is Martin Plunkett."

"What sort of company is it?" asked Shadow.

Jimmy shrugged as he retrieved two more pieces of paper covered in his tiny scrawl. "From what I can tell, it's just a front. I think it's a way of indirectly getting money from

Alfred to Martin Plunkett. I've looked at the company accounts and Plunkett takes a pretty hefty director's salary each year."

Shadow began studying the rows of figures Jimmy laid out in front of him, as his sergeant continued to explain.

"You see, Chief, I also looked back at the minutes from council committee meetings. At least the committees Plunkett sits on, planning and city retail and tourism, the two really useful ones. The payments Alfred made tie in almost perfectly to decisions those two council committees made that were favourable to Alfred."

Shadow rested his chin on his hands and absorbed all the information Jimmy had given him. Suddenly all the decisions taken by the council that he had considered dubious, from where the Viking Festival was held, to the building on the land around Battlefield Farm, started to make sense.

"There's more, Chief," continued Jimmy. "Did Sophie catch up with you about the coroner's report on Agnetha's death?"

"Yes, she did. Actually, I might have been a bit short with her," he admitted, reflecting on their earlier conversation.

Jimmy raised an eyebrow. "Don't worry about it, Chief. She knows what you're like."

"What do you mean?" asked Shadow, bristling.

"Well, I warned her you hated to be interrupted when you were eating. I expect she gave as good as she got. Did she tell you the bit about Martin Plunkett signing the report? He was the city's coroner at the time and, as you know, Agnetha died not long after Alfred discovered the Fulford Hoard."

Shadow raised an eyebrow as he realised what Jimmy was implying and what Edward had mentioned.

"By law, any treasure found has to be reported to the coroner within fourteen days," he added.

"Exactly." Jimmy grinned. "I bet that's when Alfred and Martin started working together, but I haven't gone back that far yet."

"You keep digging," agreed Shadow. "Heaven only knows how long all this corruption has been going on for."

"Do you think Plunkett might be involved with the murders too, Chief?"

"I don't know," admitted Shadow. "I suppose we need to find out if Alfred was more valuable to him alive or dead. Does the money dry up now he has gone or is there a way Plunkett can get his hands on more of it? Maybe Chloe's arrival changed the dynamic of their relationship more than he admitted to me."

He turned to look at the whiteboard where pictures of those involved in the case – victims, witnesses, and suspects – were all pinned up. Alfred and Chloe were in the centre and surrounded by Dan, Edward, Will, Annabel, and now the recently added: Bjorn and Plunkett.

"By the way," he asked, "any news about Bjorn?"

Jimmy looked up from his computer screen and slapped

his hand against his forehead.

"Sorry, Chief! I completely forgot, I was so caught up in all this stuff about Plunkett. Uniform picked Bjorn up in the early hours this morning. He was staggering around down Micklegate. Right now, he's down in the cells, but we can't interview him until he's sobered up."

"Oh, perfect!" grumbled Shadow. He imagined a hungover Bjorn would be like interviewing a bear with a sore head.

"What do you think he and Plunkett were arguing about when you heard them in the Mucky Duck?"

Shadow shifted in his chair. He didn't want to confess he'd been too distracted to hear most of the conversation.

"From what you've told me, I think Plunkett persuaded Bjorn to break into the duplex and steal Alfred's financial papers when he knew he was dead. Remember, he was the first person Edward told. Now, Plunket was either angry because Bjorn was too heavy-handed and had attracted our attention or Bjorn was trying to be clever and blackmailing him with all the info he'd stolen."

"If Plunkett did want Alfred dead, he could have involved Bjorn in that too. After all, his company was responsible for security at the Viking Festival," added Jimmy.

At that moment, Tom, the eager young constable who had been posted outside Ragnar's Palace, put his head round the door. "Sorry to interrupt, sir, but the chief constable is on the phone for you."

"Tell her I'm not here," replied Shadow automatically.

Tom gave Jimmy a worried glance.

"You should probably take it, Chief," suggested Jimmy. "When she called earlier, she said if she didn't speak to you before lunch today, she would assume you were on holiday – permanently."

"All right, put her through then," sighed Shadow as he picked up the telephone on the desk next to him and waited to hear the chief constable's high, piercing voice. As usual, Shadow found he was not required to contribute much to these conversations with his boss. He balanced the telephone receiver between his ear and his shoulder, browsing through some of Jimmy's notes, as she proceeded to give him a lecture on the need for expediency in the Alfred and Chloe case.

"The cancellation of the Viking Festival has had a huge impact on the local economy. The leaders of the city council want answers. I shouldn't need to remind you that Alfred Campbell had some friends in very high places, Shadow, and they want his killer brought to justice."

Shadow didn't think this was the time to tell her that at least one of those friends in high places was about to come crashing down to earth. The loud click of the receiver being replaced at the other end of the line told him the lecture was over. He glanced across to Jimmy, who was rubbing his eyes and yawning widely. Shadow stood up and pulled on his old wax jacket.

"Come on, I think we both need some fresh air and I'll even buy you one of those overpriced coffees you like."

As the two of them left the station, Tom called out from behind the reception desk.

"If there are any more calls while you are out, I'll leave the messages on your desk, Chief Inspector."

"Thank you, Constable," replied Shadow, then lowering his voice: "He's very keen, isn't he?"

"Tom has hopes of joining CID, Chief." Jimmy smiled.

"More fool him," murmured Shadow.

THE TWO DETECTIVES stepped out into St Helen's Square. It was a bright sunny day and the square was crowded with tourists. There was also the unmistakable sound of jingling bells and an accordion playing.

"For crying out loud! This is all I need!" groaned Shadow.

"I take it you're not a fan of morris dancing, Chief?"

Shadow shook his head grimly. "I despair sometimes. The French have the cancan, the Spanish have flamenco, the Austrians the waltz and what do we have? Morris dancing. Middle-aged men with bells and ribbons on their ankles skipping about waving hankies and tapping sticks together." Shadow took out his wallet and handed a ten-pound note to Jimmy. "You go and get the drinks. I'll wait for you down

Stonegate. I can't stay here listening to this. Oh, and if I were you, I'd order an espresso."

Jimmy disappeared into his favourite coffee shop. Shadow attempted to edge his way around the clapping crowd when he suddenly heard some very heavy panting behind him and felt something cold and wet press against his hand. He turned around in surprise to find Maggie and Harald standing there. It was hard to tell which of them was more out of breath.

"This dog will be the death of me," Maggie gasped and pointed a finger at Shadow, "and I've got a bone to pick with you."

"Why? What have I done?" asked Shadow, slightly taken aback. Maggie might be small, but she could be fierce.

"A few nights back, I had a window at the shop smashed."

"Well, I'm very sorry, Maggie, but that's hardly my fault," Shadow began.

"Wait, I haven't finished." She paused again to catch her breath. "The window was bad enough, but one of your lot spotted it and called out someone to fix it."

"It's our job to prevent looting. It's the responsible thing for a police officer on patrol to do," Shadow tried to explain.

"Not when that company then charges me two hundred and fifty quid! Talk about daylight robbery! It was only a tiny window and who on earth is going to loot a laundry? What are they going to take? A lot of dirty washing? And as far as I am concerned, John Shadow, you're an accessory!"

Without giving Shadow a chance to respond, Maggie and Harald pushed past sending tourists and morris dancers scattering.

"Crikey! Who's rattled her cage?" asked Jimmy, appearing again with two cups of coffee.

"It seems she's the latest victim of your supposed protection racket." Shadow briefly relayed what Maggie had told him. "Didn't any of the other business owners complain about the cost of their windows being fixed?"

"No, they were just grateful nothing had been stolen. I think most planned on claiming on their insurance," explained Jimmy between sips of coffee.

"You'd better find out which company has the contract for emergency call-outs."

They began walking down Stonegate towards the Minster. Jimmy rapidly started tapping away on his phone. Shadow was always amazed his deputy didn't bump into things as he walked along, engrossed by his little screen. A few seconds later, Jimmy gave a grunt of surprise.

"You'll never believe it, Chief!"

"What?"

"It's AAB Security!"

"Bjorn Bennington's company? I can well believe it. And who decided to give the contract to him?"

"I know that answer already. It's decided by the retail and tourism committee, and guess who's in charge of that committee?"

"Martin Plunkett."

"Right first time, Chief."

"Sergeant, this is a serious investigation. Can you try not to make it sound like a game show!"

"Sorry, Chief."

"Anyway, the two of them have certainly got plenty of questions to answer." Shadow frowned as they approached the Minster. He hated the idea that his uniformed officers, trying to do their job, had become involved in what was clearly a scam. A scam that had now targeted an old friend of his.

"So, do you think Bjorn smashed all the windows himself?" asked Jimmy as they turned towards Goodramgate. "I've been adding it up and he must have made over two and a half grand on call-outs."

Shadow nodded, but his mind was elsewhere.

"I think we need to do something to make it up to Maggie," he announced abruptly.

Jimmy looked at him in surprise. "It's not like you to be sentimental, Chief."

Shadow scowled. "It's not sentimental to try and repair the reputation of our fellow officers, Sergeant."

"Flowers?" Jimmy suggested as they walked past a florist's shop. Shadow shook his head impatiently.

"You really do have no imagination, Sergeant. This is precisely why you should read more books. Anyway, I've had a better idea, something Maggie will appreciate much more than flowers."

They arrived at Maggie's laundry and stepped through the door to be greeted with a loud "Woof!" Harald had his paws up on the counter. As Shadow had predicted, on his hind legs, he was much taller than Maggie. She looked up and pointed to a small pane of glass that had an equally small piece of cardboard taped over it.

"That's all they did! They didn't even replace the glass."

Shadow and Jimmy could see why she was cross.

"We can understand you being upset, Maggie, even though the officers were just doing their jobs, so we thought of something to help. Sergeant Chang here has kindly offered to take over walking Harald for you," Shadow announced.

Jimmy, who was stood behind him, let out an almost inaudible whimper. Shadow purposely did not look around. However, Maggie's face immediately broke into a broad smile as she turned to Jimmy.

"Is that true, love? It's very kind of you. He's too much for me to manage."

"No problem at all, Mrs Jackson," replied Jimmy with a rigid smile. Harald barked in approval and Maggie came bustling out from behind the counter to give Jimmy a hug.

"I knew you must have a heart of gold to put up with this old misery," she said, nudging Shadow playfully with her elbow. Now it was the chief inspector's turn to give an awkward smile.

"Good, well, that's all sorted then," he said. "Bring Harald round when you close tonight, and Sergeant Chang will exercise him."

THE TWO DETECTIVES said goodbye to a much happier Maggie and stepped outside.

"Now, don't get upset," said Shadow as soon as they were out of hearing distance.

"You could have asked first, Chief," complained Jimmy.

"You might have said no. Anyway, what's the problem? You go running every day; now you'll have Harald to keep you company. Besides, it's good PR. Think of all the people Maggie will tell about the nice young sergeant who's helping her out."

Before Jimmy could protest any further, his phone began bleeping.

"Anything important?" asked Shadow as they headed back to the station.

"I'm not sure, Chief," replied Jimmy. "It's a bit weird. The owner of the toy shop, who had their window smashed a few days ago, has sent me a text. It says the soft toy that was stolen has been returned. It was left on the doorstep with a note."

"That is strange," agreed Shadow. "Where did you say the toy shop was?"

"Lord Mayor's Walk. Just around the corner, Chief."

"Let's go and take a look."

Jimmy looked at him in astonishment. Up until now, Shadow had been dismissive, to say the least, when it came to the spate of broken windows.

"Do you think there's a connection between the smashed windows and the murders?" he asked as two men turned and retraced their steps back down Goodramgate.

"I want to have as much information as possible for when Bjorn is sober enough to be interviewed. Also, when the names of two men keep cropping up during a murder investigation, we should follow all avenues – even ones that lead us to teddy bears."

"It was a blue fluffy rabbit actually, Chief."

"Very amusing, Sergeant," replied Shadow. Something Jimmy had said was bothering him, but he could not think why.

THEY WALKED BENEATH Monk Bar, one of the ancient gateways in the city walls and turned left on to Lord Mayor's Walk. The toy shop was painted in bright blue and pink stripes. Mary Shuttleworth opened it over thirty years ago and had been selling dolls and cuddly toys to the children of York ever since. Mary Shuttleworth herself was a jolly-looking woman whose grey curly hair was coloured a pale shade of lilac. She looked delighted to see Jimmy again when they walked through the door.

"Oh, hello, love. Are you all right? Did you get my text message?" she asked, enveloping Jimmy in a huge hug.

Shadow raised an eyebrow. His sergeant's uncanny ability to become best friends with most of the people he met never failed to astonish him.

"Yes, thank you, Mrs Shuttleworth," Jimmy said, flushing pink with embarrassment. "This is Chief Inspector Shadow."

"Good morning, Mrs Shuttleworth," said Shadow, nodding politely.

"Hello, Chief Inspector, are you Sergeant Chang's boss? You know he was so kind and helpful when my window was broken. He's a real credit to the force."

"I'm pleased to hear it," replied Shadow, but Mrs Shuttleworth had turned her attention back to Jimmy.

"When you left last time, you told me to let you know if I had any more information, so I thought I should tell you. It was very strange. I arrived this morning, as usual, to open up and there he was sitting on the doorstep." She pointed to a big blue fluffy rabbit sitting on her counter. Shadow stepped forward to take a closer look at him.

"Your text mentioned that there was also a note left?" Jimmy queried.

"Yes, there was, Sergeant." Mrs Shuttleworth squeezed herself between two large boxes to get behind the counter to the large old-fashioned cash register. She pressed a button, the drawer pinged open, and she retrieved a folded piece of lined paper.

"Here it is. I put it in the till for safekeeping. I thought about putting it in a little plastic bag, you know like you see on those detective shows on television, for evidence, but when I looked at the writing, I thought it was probably just kids messing about."

She handed the paper to Jimmy, who unfolded it and read the message. The writing was an uneven childish scrawl in pencil and said simply, *"I am very sorry I took your rabbit. I won't do it again."* Jimmy showed it to Shadow, who read it in silence, folded it, and then tucked it into his pocket.

"You don't mind if I hold on to it, do you, Mrs Shuttleworth?" he asked.

"Of course not, dear, not if you think it's important." She smiled. "Now, can I make you two gentlemen a nice cup of tea? I've got a lovely Sicilian lemon drizzle cake in the back. I only made it last night."

"That's very kind of you. I'd love a piece, but unfortunately Sergeant Chang needs to go and fetch a car round," replied Shadow.

"Do I, Chief?" asked Jimmy. It was the first he had heard of the idea.

"Yes, off you go," said Shadow, waving his hand dismissively.

TEN MINUTES, OR one cup of tea and two slices of cake later, Jimmy pulled up outside the shop, looking disgruntled. Shadow waved Mrs Shuttleworth goodbye and slid into the passenger seat.

"Do you mind telling me where we're going, Chief?" Jimmy asked.

"Battlefield Farm, Fulford."

"I thought we were going after Martin Plunkett?" Normally, Jimmy didn't bother querying instructions, but Shadow guessed being volunteered as a dog walker combined with lack of sleep, and now deprived of cake, was beginning to test even Jimmy's easy-going nature.

"We will, but first I want to speak with Will Campbell. I remember seeing him with a blue rabbit on the sofa when we first met him. Any news back at the station?"

"Tom said there were some messages for you, so I told him to text me if they were important."

A few minutes later, they came to a halt outside the farmhouse.

"You wait here, I won't be long," instructed Shadow as he stepped out of the car. This needed to be a delicate visit. They couldn't go in heavy-handed. He was almost at the front door when he remembered something, went back to the car, and leant in through Jimmy's lowered window.

"I almost forgot. Mrs Shuttleworth insisted," he said,

handing over the slightly squashed slice of lemon drizzle wrapped in a pink napkin. "Between her and Maggie, you've got the makings of your own fan club, Sergeant." He grinned.

AS HE ENTERED the kitchen at Battlefield Farm, once again he was met with loud barking and the delicious smell of home cooking. There were several large pans bubbling away on top of the Aga and deep dishes of what looked like cottage and shepherd's pies lined up on the table.

"Crikey!" exclaimed Shadow. "You look like you're preparing to feed an army marching to war!"

"No, Chief Inspector, just two very hungry sons who can't cook." Annabel Campbell smiled. "I'm filling up the freezer."

Shadow nodded. Judging by their size, he imagined it would take a lot to feed Dan and Will. Annabel herself certainly couldn't eat very much. She was as thin as a rake.

"I need to speak with Will about the soft toy he took," said Shadow, deciding to be direct. Besides, he got the distinct feeling Annabel had been expecting him. He was right. She was equally direct.

"I don't know what got into him," she said, wiping her hands on her apron before placing them on her hips. "He does know right from wrong, Chief Inspector. I have always made sure of that. When I realised he had taken it, I told him he had to give it back and say sorry."

Shadow nodded, relieved that she wasn't going to pretend she didn't know what he was talking about.

"What did he say to you about it?"

"Not much, which is strange as well. It's not like him to be secretive. He only said he had been out one night looking for the peregrine falcon when he saw the broken window and took the rabbit. He does love rabbits," she added with a small smile. "Is he in a lot of trouble?" Annabel's forehead was now furrowed, and she was twisting the edge of her apron nervously as she spoke.

"The shop owner isn't planning on pressing charges," he explained. While he spoke, Shadow noticed Will outside the kitchen window. He was carefully filling the bird feeders up with peanuts. There was still a bandage on his hand.

"I would still like to speak to him though."

"Very well, Chief Inspector, but please go gently with him," Annabel implored him. She quickly rinsed her hands at the sink and dried them on her apron.

"You lot stay!" she commanded the three wagging dogs as she opened the back door and ushered Shadow through.

When Shadow stepped outside, Will looked up in surprise. Then surprise turned to panic. Shadow gave him what he hoped was a reassuring smile.

"Mr Shadow needs to speak with you, Will," said Annabel simply.

"It's okay, Will. You're not in any trouble. I only want to have a quick chat," Shadow said. "You did the right thing taking the rabbit back. I would like to ask you three questions – that's all, just three."

Despite Shadow trying to sound as calm as possible, terror filled the young man's face. What was making him so scared? Shadow wondered. Will turned and walked towards an old stable. Shadow turned to Annabel, who motioned with a nod of her head that they should follow him.

The inside of the stable felt dark compared to the bright glare of the sun outside and there was a not unpleasant smell of hay and dog biscuits. An old paint-splattered table stood against the wall with large bags of bird feed and peanuts and on the floor were several sacks of dried dog food. One corner was partitioned off with a makeshift wall made of stepladders and folded deckchairs and there were several towels and a large cardboard box behind it.

Annabel stood quietly in the doorway and Will was by the table fiddling with a box of cat treats. Shadow tried again.

"Don't worry, Will, you don't have to say anything. Please just nod your head for yes or shake it for no, okay?"

Will nodded his head without looking up.

"Good. Now, did you cut your hand on the broken shop window?"

Will nodded again.

"And was somebody else there when you took the blue

rabbit, someone who told you it was okay to take it?"

Another nod.

"The person who was there, did they tell you something bad would happen if you spoke about any of this?"

Will looked up very quickly and met Shadow's eyes then glanced away but nodded again. It was as Shadow had guessed. The bully had found another victim. He was tempted to ask more questions but didn't want to break his promise to the frightened young man.

"That's perfect, thank you very much, Will."

He was about to leave Will in peace when he noticed a pretty ginger cat creep out of the box behind the barricade. Shadow reached down to stroke her, but she hissed loudly and swiped at him with her paw. Shadow quickly withdrew his hand.

"Don't mind Toffee, Mr Shadow," said Will softly. "She's just protecting her babies."

Sure enough, as Shadow cautiously peered inside the box, he could see one tabby and two ginger kittens.

"Good boy, Will," said Annabel and she led Shadow back to the house. Before leaving he assured her this would be the end of the matter.

As INSTRUCTED, JIMMY was still waiting in the car outside, studying the screen of his phone intently.

"I've got good news and bad news, Chief," he announced as Shadow slammed the car door shut. "Bjorn has sobered up, but we still can't interview him."

"Why not?" asked Shadow. The list of questions he had for young Mr Bennington was getting longer by the minute.

"His brief hasn't turned up."

"Did he use his telephone call to contact them? Who is it?"

"It's Martin Plunkett, Chief. When the custody sergeant called his office to see why he hadn't arrived, they said he'd gone home early."

"Early?" said Shadow, looking at his watch. "It's only half past eleven in the morning! Do we have his home address?"

Jimmy rapidly pressed a few buttons on his phone. "Yes, Thorn Nook in Heworth."

"Well, let's head over there."

"Okay, Chief," replied Jimmy as he turned on the ignition. "Oh and Tom also said someone called Hugo, from Guernsey, has being trying to get hold of you."

"Is Hugo his first or last name?" asked Shadow.

"No idea, Chief."

"Well, whoever he is, he'll have to wait until we catch up with Plunkett," Shadow said through gritted teeth as Jimmy sped away.

HEWORTH WAS ON the other side of the city, a suburb to the north of York. Thorn Nook was an exclusive row of houses situated behind Heworth Golf Course. Jimmy turned into the cul-de-sac and slowly drove past the large mock Tudor houses hidden behind high privet hedges.

"Which one is it?" asked Shadow, peering out of the passenger window.

"Number five, Chief, but I'm not sure which end they start numbering from," replied Jimmy, who had now reached the end of the lane and was beginning to make a three-point turn. "We'll have to look again."

Suddenly there was the roar of an engine and a gold car sped out of one of the driveways.

"It's him," said Shadow.

"You sure, Chief?"

"Definitely, I remember his car – it's got a private reg. Get after him."

Jimmy didn't need to be asked twice. He spun the steering wheel, slammed his foot down on the accelerator, and raced off after Plunkett's car. However, when they got to the junction by the golf club, there was no sign of him.

"Okay, Chief, which way – left or right?" asked Jimmy.

"Left," said Shadow decisively. "At the speed he was going, I get the feeling he wants to get out of the city. I certainly don't think he was dashing to Bjorn's assistance."

It was strange that Bjorn had called the solicitor when Plunkett had told him not to contact him again. Was Bjorn asking for his help or warning him?

Jimmy turned their car towards the ring road and sure enough, a few seconds later, they could see the gold car in the distance, waiting at traffic lights.

"Put a call out," instructed Shadow.

Jimmy radioed all the cars in the area with the description and number plate details of the car they were following. "Siren?" he asked hopefully. They were in an unmarked car, but it came equipped with a flashing light and siren.

As the gold car sped away from the traffic lights, Shadow sighed. "I suppose so, if you must."

A few seconds later, the siren was blaring and the light now on top of their car was flashing bright blue. Jimmy began weaving through the traffic and Shadow's knuckles grew whiter as his fingers clung on to the sides of his seat. Martin continued to speed through several roundabouts on the outer ring road.

"You think he's seen us, Chief?" asked Jimmy, raising his voice above the sound of the siren.

"I'm sure he has," replied Shadow through gritted teeth.

"You think he'll pull over?"

Shadow shook his head. "No, I don't, and you know what they say – the innocent don't run."

By now they had reached the A64, the main road that linked the east coast of Yorkshire to Leeds. To Shadow's surprise, Martin took the turning for Scarborough at the junction.

"I thought he'd head to Leeds, maybe try to get a flight out of the country," he said, thinking out loud.

"Oh, I think he's trying to get out of the country, Chief. Remember I said the *Agnetha* is moored at the marina in Scarborough? What if he's got the keys Bjorn used to get into the duplex and there's a set for the boat?"

Shadow glanced across to his sergeant and saw the broad grin on his face.

"Then let's hope we catch him before he gets there. If he ends up sailing off to France or Spain, we'll have to get Interpol on the case."

"Yes, Chief," replied Jimmy, trying hard to sound serious.

Shadow smiled to himself. He knew perfectly well high-speed chases and tracking down international criminals were the thing Jimmy dreamed of instead of taking notes and wandering the streets of York. They were now several miles away from York, and Plunkett was showing no signs of slowing down.

In the rear-view mirror, Shadow could see more blue flashing lights of a marked car coming to join them and as they passed the slip road for Malton, another marked car from the market town slipped in behind. Jimmy accelerated again, speeding past a startled-looking tractor driver.

"We need to stop him before he gets to Scarborough," said Shadow over the radio to the other cars. Plunkett's driving was becoming increasingly erratic as he swerved through the traffic. It was dangerous enough here on a dual carriageway, but if he reached the busy seaside town, it could be lethal.

Following his instructions, the patrol car from Malton accelerated sharply. Its sirens blaring, it tore ahead of the other cars. The officer's crackling voice came over the radio. "If you can get him down the slip road to Yedingham, we'll deploy the stinger, sir."

On hearing this idea, Jimmy veered to the right, so he was now alongside Plunkett, and the patrol car from York came up behind, so the two of them were almost corralling the gold car. Shadow, in the passenger seat, was now close enough to see Plunkett's sweaty hands as they gripped the steering wheel. He watched as the solicitor's eyes kept nervously flickering to look in the rear-view mirror.

The three cars raced past the sign showing the turning for Yedingham was at the next junction. As they had hoped, Plunkett recklessly swung his car without any warning to the left, off the dual carriageway and towards the village. He obviously thought he had more chance of losing the police down a quiet, narrow country lane, not wide enough for two cars. However, the other patrol car was waiting for him, with the stinger already out across the road.

"We've got him now, Chief," said Jimmy, who, unlike his boss, was thoroughly enjoying the chase. Plunkett saw the stinger and tried to swerve, but he was too late. His tyres tore as they hit its sharp teeth and the car came to an abrupt halt.

Jimmy and the other patrol car skidded to a stop behind him.

The two uniformed officers from Malton rushed forward and hauled Plunkett out of his seat. He was looking dazed, having been hit in the face when his airbag deployed. Jimmy hurried over to handcuff him and read him his rights. Meanwhile, Shadow climbed out too, feeling a little shaky from Jimmy's driving, and went to investigate what was in the boot of Plunkett's car. He opened it to find a holdall and two briefcases. The holdall contained a few clothes and personal effects, but the suitcases were both full of cash. When he raised his head again, he could hear Plunkett loudly complaining.

"Chief Inspector, this a terrible mistake. I've done nothing wrong," he pleaded.

"You can tell me all about it back at the station, Mr Plunkett," replied Shadow and he motioned to the uniformed officers from York. "Take him away."

He watched as they put Plunkett, still protesting, into the back of their marked car. Then, while Jimmy loaded the contents of Plunkett's boot into the back of their own car, Shadow went to thank the constable and sergeant from Malton for their assistance and ask them to arrange to have Plunkett's car removed from the lane.

"We were happy to help, Chief Inspector Shadow," replied the sergeant. "There is one other thing I wanted to mention. It may or may not be important."

"Go ahead, Sergeant," said Shadow.

"When we were given the details of the car you were in pursuit of, the reg number rang a bell, so we checked back, and something came up. Two nights ago, Scarborough police got reports of a gold car with the same private number. The driver was behaving suspiciously down by the harbour. A patrol car was sent to investigate, but when the officers arrived the car had gone."

"I see, well, thank you again, Sergeant, that could be very useful."

Shadow also nodded his thanks to the constable and returned to the car.

"Ready to go home, Chief?" Jimmy asked as Shadow pulled his seat belt on.

"Not quite yet," replied Shadow. "We're going to have a trip to the seaside after all. Try to remember we're not chasing anyone now, so stick to the speed limit."

CHAPTER EIGHT

Across 5 (9 letters)
Playing a children's game, you must bluff when wearing this

SCARBOROUGH WAS ONLY a twenty-minute drive further along the A64. Once just a sleepy fishing village, it had become a fashionable resort for the Victorians who wanted to escape the dirty industrial cities and enjoy the bracing North Sea air. Over the years it had gradually lost its popularity due to the availability of cheap package holidays to the continent where, unlike Yorkshire, the sunshine was guaranteed. However, on this cool, but sunny September day there were still plenty of older couples strolling arm in arm along the promenade, enjoying fish and chips wrapped in newspaper or ice creams in cones.

Jimmy pulled into the harbour car park and the two detectives stepped out. They were greeted by the unmistakable salty smell of the sea and the screech of seagulls circling overhead. Shadow took a deep breath. It was years since he had been to the coast. They began walking along the harbour wall that jutted out into the sea.

"How will we find the *Agnetha*, Chief?" asked Jimmy.

"I don't think that's going to be difficult, Sergeant," replied Shadow and he pointed out towards the lighthouse at the end of the harbour wall. Moored there was a huge white motor yacht. It stood out like a sore thumb amongst the modest fishing boats and hard-working trawlers. As they got closer, the *Agnetha*'s sleek lines and shining chrome gleaming in the sun looked even more impressive.

"Wow!" exclaimed Jimmy. "I bet it's worth even more than his duplex."

They both took one look at the beautifully polished wooden deck and removed their shoes before climbing aboard. Jimmy began trying each of the keys they had found in Plunkett's bag while Shadow watched two spaniels chasing each other along the beach, yapping happily.

"We're in, Chief," declared Jimmy as he finally found the right key. They stepped inside and found the interior was even more impressive than the outside of the boat. There were thick cream carpets, deep suede sofas, and a polished wooden, very well-stocked bar. Shadow, who had lived on a boat for nearly thirty years, had to admit this craft was in a different league to *Florence* and her cosy cabins.

"What are we looking for, Chief?" asked Jimmy.

Shadow gave a shrug. "I'm not sure, but there must have been a good reason for Plunkett coming here in the middle of the night. I'll have a poke around here, while you go and check the bedrooms."

After only a few seconds, Jimmy called out, "In here, Chief!"

Shadow followed the sound of his sergeant's voice and found him in one of the bedrooms. He was almost dazzled as he stepped inside. The sun streaming through the window was bouncing off the mirrors on the walls and ceiling. The presence of many leopard-print cushions scattered about made him think this must have been Alfred and Chloe's room. Jimmy was peering into a black holdall lying on the gold satin sheet covering the bed.

"What have you found?" asked Shadow.

"I didn't want to touch it, Chief, but it looks to be full of Viking stuff." Jimmy stepped aside so Shadow could take a look. The bag was indeed crammed with Viking "stuff". There was a helmet, a couple of daggers, several drinking vessels, jewellery, coins, and the thing that really caught Shadow's attention: a "Cats of Freya" bangle.

"No wonder Miss Treanor couldn't find it in any museum," he murmured.

"Do you think these are the real thing or replicas? Some of it looks pretty old and rusty," said Jimmy.

"Check that Daneholm, Alfred's Viking museum, isn't missing anything," instructed Shadow. "Plunkett is one of the directors there. He could easily have accessed it."

Jimmy quickly made a call to the museum and spoke with the assistant he had met previously, while Shadow paced up and down thinking. He had a feeling the items they had discovered had been missing for much longer than a few days.

"All present and correct, Chief. Nothing's missing," Jimmy reported, slipping the phone back into his pocket.

"Then let's get all this back to the station, so we can have Stan and Ollie check it out," he said without thinking.

Jimmy gave him a quizzical look. "It's Ben remember, Chief? Wouldn't Edward Bennington or someone at the museum be able to tell us more?"

"No doubt, but until we know who is or isn't involved in all of this, I think we need to keep it in-house. You load it into the car and lock up here," said Shadow, heading towards the door.

"No problem, Chief. Where are you going?"

"To get us some lunch. We can't come to Scarborough and not have fish and chips."

BY THE TIME the two detectives returned to the station, it was mid-afternoon.

"Do you want me to sit in on the interviews with you, Chief?" asked Jimmy.

Shadow shook his head. "No thanks, Jimmy. You go to forensics and then get back to that computer of yours. Keep looking into those bank accounts, particularly the offshore ones. When we do charge Plunkett, I want to be able to throw the book at him. Oh, and find out what the chap from Guernsey wanted."

YORK POLICE STATION was housed in the old Medieval Guildhall by the river. The custody suites, as they now called the cells and interview rooms, were in the basement. No matter what they named it or how bright they made the lighting, the place still had the aura of its original purpose: a dark, dank dungeon to hold the city's outlaws. As Shadow made his way down the steep twisting stone steps, he almost bumped into Astrid coming up the other way.

"Good afternoon, are you here to see Bjorn?" he asked, a little surprised to see her. The last time they had met he had gained the impression there was no love lost between the half-siblings.

"Hello, Chief Inspector. I was, but apparently I'm not needed."

"Really? Why is that?" he asked.

Astrid shrugged. "Who knows with Bjorn. I admit I'm not a specialist in criminal law, but I thought he'd be pleased to see a friendly face, at least until his own solicitor, whoever that is, turned up." Shadow noted mentally that Bjorn hadn't told her he'd called Plunkett as Astrid continued to talk. "However, I was charmingly told to 'get lost', so I am doing as my client instructed." She began to climb the stairs again, when Shadow thought of something and called out after her.

"Hold on a minute, Astrid!"

She paused and turned back.

"Why did you want to read about the inquest into your mother's death?" he asked.

"How did you find out about that? Wait, are you looking into my mother's death too?" Her eyes were bright, and she sounded very eager all of a sudden.

"Not exactly," replied Shadow, not wanting to reveal too much to her at this stage.

Astrid raked her fingers through her hair as her shoulders drooped. Shadow felt quite sorry for her.

"I was only five when she died, and Dad still can't bring himself to talk about it. He'll occasionally mention a song she liked or something funny she said, but he clams up whenever I try to ask him anything."

Shadow nodded sympathetically. His mother had barely spoken about his father either.

"I've always wanted to find out exactly what happened. So much doesn't make sense. I am sure Martin Plunkett knows more. Did you know he conducted the inquest? I've approached him several times, but he won't speak to me. Is it true you are holding him here too?" She looked over his shoulder back towards the cells.

"If we do hear something about you mother, you'll be the first to know," Shadow reassured her, without confirming or denying anything.

Astrid sighed. "Thank you, Chief Inspector," she said a little sadly, then gave him a brief wave goodbye before she disappeared up the steps.

WHEN SHADOW ENTERED the custody suite, he was surprised to see George sitting behind the desk.

"What are you doing down here?" he asked. George was usually to be found in the records office in the top of the Guildhall tower.

"The two lads who are usually down here are both off sick, so I volunteered to cover, for my sins," he joked.

"Anything to report?" asked Shadow.

George shook his head. "Not really. Plunkett has been processed. He has also been loudly protesting his innocence to anyone who will listen since he arrived. Meanwhile, Bennington junior just sent his sister packing."

"Half-sister," said Shadow automatically. He turned to get himself a coffee from the drinks dispenser in the corner, but it had disappeared.

"What's happened to the drinks machine?" he asked.

George pointed to an electric coffee pot bubbling away at the end of his desk and a pile of neatly stacked cups and saucers. "It's gone on the orders of the chief constable. All part of her new green initiative. Apparently, we were using too many plastic cups, so it's back to the old-fashioned way."

Shadow sighed as he poured out two cups of coffee. As much as he wanted to help save the planet, he couldn't help thinking the chief constable should have more important things to focus on other than their drinks machine. He didn't want to speak to Plunkett until he'd heard from Jimmy, so he walked across to the first interview room and peeked through the small window in the door. Bjorn was still sitting at the small white table glowering at Tom, who was trying his best not to look nervous. Shadow caught the eye of the young constable and nodded to him. Tom hurried over and opened the door for the chief inspector.

"Thank you, Tom. I think I can take it from here," Shadow said.

"Yes, sir," replied Tom, looking relieved as he scuttled out, closing the door behind him. Shadow placed the two cups of coffee on the table and sat down in the chair opposite Bjorn. The young man folded his arms and pushed his chair back with his feet. His eyes were bloodshot, his T-shirt stained, and he stank of stale beer.

"I told you before, I don't drink with coppers."

Shadow nodded and calmly took a sip of his coffee. "That's fine, Bjorn. I'll drink; you can talk."

"You can't interview me without my brief. I've got rights," he said defensively.

"But you sent your solicitor away, so I assumed you were waiving that right."

Bjorn's upper lip curled into a snarl. "She wasn't my solicitor. She's my useless sister. All she does is divorces and wills and stuff. Besides, she'd probably want to see me

169

stitched up. Where's Plunkett? That's who I called."

"Unfortunately, Martin Plunkett will not be able to act for you. We arrested him about an hour ago."

Bjorn did not react with any surprise to this news. Shadow wondered fleetingly if Astrid had told him this, or he expected it anyway.

"What have you arrested him for?"

"Bjorn, I take it you haven't forgotten that I am investigating the murders of Alfred and Chloe Campbell?"

This time the young man paused. "You think Plunkett killed them?"

"I think the two of you have been working together for some time. For example, when the council committee, under Plunkett's direction, awarded your business the contract to respond to emergency call-outs and then the security for the Viking Festival. You must have been pleased. That's a great start for a new business like yours."

Bjorn gave Shadow an unpleasant, taunting smile. "You know what they say, Mr Shadow. It's not what you know, it's who you know."

Shadow got the feeling the young man thought he was being clever. He was almost showing off. "You paid Plunkett for those contracts?"

"He got his cut all right." He shrugged. "That's how it works round here."

"I see." Shadow nodded. "Is that also why you did him such a big favour? Why on the night Alfred died, at Plunkett's request, you stole his keys, entered his apartment, and took financial papers from his office?"

"No, I didn't. I don't care what Plunkett says. It's my word against his. You've got no proof!"

"On the contrary, we found a very clear fingerprint belonging to you."

Bjorn's eyes flashed dangerously. "You liar, I never touched that filing cabinet."

Shadow gave a slight, sardonic smile. Bjorn might be tough, but he certainly wasn't very bright.

"And I never mentioned it."

Bjorn stared at him, his mouth slightly open, and confusion in his eyes. "Yes, you did," he shouted. "You just said!"

Shadow shook his head calmly. "No, I said papers had been taken from the office, that's all. Incidentally, we did find your thumbprint on the drinks' fridge, which, in your greed, you also tried to break into."

Bjorn stood up and began pacing back and forth like a caged wild animal. Shadow was unfazed. He had encountered hundreds of young men like Bjorn over the years. He took another sip of coffee before continuing.

"Now, speaking of your greed. When you went to take Alfred's keys you also helped yourself to the cash in his wallet, then threw the wallet on the fire to destroy any trace of your prints. Stealing from a dead man? You must be so proud of yourself!

"Then when you had the bank statements in your possession, you did not hand them over to Mr Plunkett, as agreed, but tried to blackmail him instead. Did you want to claw back some of the money you had paid him for helping you win the contract for being called out to replace broken windows in the city? It is a very lucrative contract, but you also chose to exploit it by smashing windows yourself."

"You've got no proof of that," interrupted Bjorn.

"Why do you think that? Perhaps because you picked on small businesses, who couldn't afford expensive surveillance equipment? You must have known such an increase in vandalism would eventually attract our attention, so you tried to be clever and get someone else to take the blame. When you spotted Will out on one of his late-night walks, you told him to take that toy knowing he was bound to cut his hand and leave blood on the window. You tried to set up that poor lad."

Bjorn gave the chief inspector another nasty smile. "I don't like your chances of convicting me if Dopey's going to be your star witness."

"Vandalism is the least of the charges I'll be bringing against you." Shadow paused briefly and held up his hand as he began counting off each of Bjorn's crimes on his fingers. "There's also theft, burglary, blackmail, and at the very least accessory to murder."

Bjorn suddenly turned very pale. "I had nothing to do with any murders. If Plunkett did, he was on his own. I only took the keys and papers like he told me to. Alfred was already dead."

Shadow drained the last of his coffee and stood up. "We shall see, won't we, Bjorn."

With that Shadow left the interview room. Tom was waiting behind the custody desk with George.

"Get him back to his cell, Constable. He's got a lot to think about."

Suddenly, there was a loud crash and the sound of breaking crockery from inside the interview room. Shadow made an educated guess that Bjorn had just thrown his cup of coffee against the wall.

"You might need to find a dustpan and brush too, Tom," he added. He thought there might be a flaw in the chief constable's new green policy, which she hadn't anticipated.

"How are you enjoying it down here?" he asked George.

"Well, it's certainly more eventful than the records office," replied his old friend, handing a piece of paper over to him. "A message from Jimmy for you," he said. "He apologised for not coming down, but said he is waiting on a call from Hugo, if that makes any sense."

Shadow read the note. Forensics had only done a brief test and really an expert opinion was needed, but the metal they tested was pre–Industrial Revolution. Shadow thought for a moment, it seemed likely the items found in the boat could be from the Viking era. He would simply have to go ahead with interviewing Plunkett and hope he would trip up as easily as Bjorn had.

"Where's Plunkett?" he asked. George, who was busy filling in a form, held two fingers up in response.

"I was only asking!"

"Very droll." George grinned as he continued writing.

Martin Plunkett was waiting for Shadow in interview room number two. Compared to his usual well-groomed appearance, he looked quite unkempt and he now had an impressive black eye from where the airbag had hit his face.

"Was it really necessary for your men to remove my tie and belt, Chief Inspector?" he demanded as soon as Shadow walked through the door, gesturing to his now open-necked shirt. Privately, Shadow thought the solicitor had a lot more to worry about than if he was properly dressed.

"They are merely following proper police procedure, Mr Plunkett," he explained. "We want to minimise the risk of anyone harming themselves while in custody."

"They even took my shoelaces," Plunkett continued to complain, showing Shadow his now unlaced shoe beneath the table.

Shadow decided to ignore him. "Have you made your phone call and contacted your solicitor, Mr Plunkett?" he asked instead.

"There's no need," Plunkett replied pompously. "I shall be representing myself in all matters. Having practised law in this city for nearly thirty years, Chief Inspector, there really isn't anyone else I would trust to do the job properly. The rest are amateurs."

Shadow thought the more likely reason was that Plunkett had made himself so unpopular with the rest of the legal fraternity, they weren't exactly queuing up to offer their assistance.

"Very well then, in that case, I shall begin our interview."

"Before you do, Chief Inspector – is my good friend Gillian aware you have arrested me?"

Shadow looked the solicitor steadily in the eye. "I spoke with the chief constable this morning. She is very keen for the investigation to progress as quickly as possible."

Plunkett didn't flinch but smiled weakly. "Then please, by all means, press on, Chief Inspector."

"Edward Bennington said he used your phone to call 999 when he found Alfred's body."

"That's right, he came hurrying out of Ragnar's Palace and almost bumped into me. The old fool wasn't wearing his glasses."

"Why were you there and not down by the river?"

"I was concerned when I realised Alfred hadn't turned up for the prize giving and went to look for him. Just like Edward."

"A few moments ago, Bjorn Bennington told me that almost as soon as Alfred's body had been discovered you asked him to break into Alfred's home and steal some financial papers."

Martin Plunkett opened his eyes very wide and spread

out his arms in a gesture of total surprise. "Bjorn was responsible for the burglary? That is a shock, Chief Inspector. Although, as I believe Bjorn does already have a criminal record, perhaps we should not be too surprised. A leopard doesn't change his spots and all that."

"If you were aware of his criminal record, why did you award him the security contract for the Viking Festival?"

"I believe everyone deserves a second chance, but you must remember it was the committee who awarded the contract, not me personally. It was a collective decision," he replied smoothly, sounding very sincere.

Shadow feared Plunkett was much cleverer and a far more accomplished liar than Bjorn. He tried again.

"Mr Plunkett, can you tell me why you refused to pull over earlier when my officers and I were pursuing you?"

"Chief Inspector, please believe me when I say I had no idea it was me you were pursuing. I saw the flashing lights and heard the sirens of course, but having done nothing wrong, it didn't cross my mind for one second that I could possibly be your intended target."

Shadow raised an eyebrow slightly. "You were heading to Scarborough?"

"Yes, Chief Inspector. It was such a beautiful day I decided to make the most of it. A quick jaunt to the seaside before winter arrives."

"I see – and do you usually take two suitcases containing approximately twenty thousand pounds with you on a day trip to the coast?"

"I had no idea they were in the car," replied Plunkett easily.

"Really? And the cache of Viking treasure we found on the *Agnetha*? You know nothing about that?"

Plunkett paused ever so slightly and licked his lips. Shadow knew he was rattled. He hadn't counted on them visiting the boat already.

"No, nothing, the *Agnetha* was Alfred's boat, not mine."

"So why was your car seen there two nights ago?"

"I simply wanted to check everything was all right. It is what Alfred would have wanted. As I told you, Chief Inspector, Alfred was a mate."

"As his mate, you must have known how close he was to Edward's wife, Agnetha, even naming his boat after her. Conducting the inquest into her death can't have been easy."

"The death of any young woman is already a tragedy, Chief Inspector."

Although he carefully hadn't accused Plunkett of anything, Shadow felt for the first time the solicitor had missed a beat. This response had been his most stilted. Shadow gave Plunkett a warm smile and pushed his chair back.

"Well, that all seems very straightforward, Mr Plunkett. Based on what you have told me, I won't expect our forensics team to find your fingerprints on any of the Viking artefacts we discovered. I'm also sure the telephone call my sergeant is currently holding with the Guernsey police won't involve you in any way."

Plunkett cleared his throat nervously and leaned across the table towards Shadow, furtively glancing around at the security cameras as he did so.

"Look, Chief Inspector, we are both men of the world. I'm sure we can come to some sort of arrangement to help you understand that all of this has just been a series of silly misunderstandings and mistakes."

Fortunately, Shadow had been in the police long enough to know when someone was attempting to bribe him. Plunkett was a man who thought every problem could be solved with grubby, underhand deals. He stood up abruptly and gave Plunkett a cold, hard stare.

"The only silly mistake you have made, Mr Plunkett, is not to get yourself proper legal representation."

HE CLOSED THE door on Plunkett and with a brief wave to George, Shadow left the custody suite and went to find Jimmy up in the incident room.

"Hi, Chief, how did the interviews go?"

Shadow shrugged, noting Jimmy was now even more upbeat than usual following the car chase.

"I think they'll both benefit from a night in the cells to come to their senses. What about you?"

Shadow pulled out a chair and sat down wearily as Jimmy tapped open his notebook with a flourish.

"I've had a very interesting chat with Inspector Hugo, from St Peter Port CID. Hugo is his surname, just so you know, Chief. Apparently, there is a wealthy Norwegian businessman named Erik Pedersen on the island. He's a shipping magnate, I think, who spends the winter months in Guernsey. He is also a well-known collector of rare Viking artefacts. It seems Plunkett had arranged to sell quite a number of items to him."

"How does Hugo know all this?" asked Shadow.

"Well, Plunkett has a girlfriend out in Guernsey called Monique. She's a local and they've been together, on and off, for quite a few years. However, on his last visit Plunkett also started seeing a young waitress from Brittany, called Sabine. Her aunt owns Plunkett's favourite restaurant, and she had been helping out there over the summer."

Shadow exhaled loudly and made an impatient turning motion with his hand. At this rate, he would have to sit through the waitress's entire family history.

Jimmy pressed on. "Now Guernsey is a very small place, so when Monique found out about Sabine, she wasn't happy and to get her own back she went to Erik Pedersen and told him the artefacts were actually undeclared treasure. Pedersen, who had already given Plunkett a down payment, didn't want to be involved in anything dodgy, so he went straight to the police."

Shadow smiled to himself. So much for Plunkett being a

man of the world. Had he never heard the old saying: "Hell hath no fury like a woman scorned"? Jimmy was still reading from his digital notebook.

"Incidentally, Chief, Pedersen has offered to send one of the experts he employs over here to look at what we found too."

"Excellent!" declared Shadow, glancing at his watch. "That's one less thing for us to do. Now, let's call it a day. I'm starving."

The sun was setting as the two detectives stepped outside the station. Shadow watched as Jimmy's good spirits also sank when they saw Maggie and Harald heading across the square towards him.

"Enjoy your walk! I'll see you back at your place." Shadow grinned, patting Jimmy on the back and waving to Maggie.

"Chief," Jimmy called after him, "Mum doesn't know about my tattoo. Don't say anything, okay?"

ONCE A WEEK, Shadow ate at the Golden Dragon, Jimmy's mother's restaurant on Goodramgate. It was in one of the oldest buildings in the city and Shadow always sat with the family on the ground floor by the kitchen, instead of the main restaurant on the first floor. Normally a solitary diner, he was surprised how much he enjoyed sitting with Jimmy's grandfather amid the hustle and bustle of customers arriving to collect takeaway orders and waitresses hurrying back and forth.

Within a few seconds of him stepping through the door, Rose – Jimmy's mother – was ready to present him with a bowl of prawn crackers and a Chinese beer. He accepted them gratefully and was about to say thank you when she fixed him with a meaningful stare.

"What do we say, Chief Inspector?" she asked.

Shadow felt himself blush. Rose had taken it upon herself to try to teach him Chinese at every opportunity.

"*Sher sher*," he muttered. It was as close as he could get to pronouncing thank you correctly. Rose beamed at him as he quickly explained the delay in her son's arrival.

Half an hour later, he stood sipping his beer and waiting at the window with Angela, Jimmy's younger sister. They both burst out laughing as an unusually stressed-looking Jimmy was dragged past by Harald on their way back to Maggie's shop. Like Jimmy's family, Maggie also lived above her business.

Shadow and Angela laughed even more when a few minutes later Jimmy staggered through the door out of breath and with his jeans covered in dog drool. Rose came hurrying out of the kitchen and reached up to take Jimmy's face in her hands.

"You poor thing! Look at the state of you." She kissed her son on the cheek and ruffled his hair. "But you are such a good boy helping Mrs Jackson like that!"

Angela rolled her eyes as her mother disappeared back into the kitchen and Jimmy went to get changed. Rose made no secret of the fact that Jimmy was her favourite child. Angela turned to her grandfather, who didn't speak English, and began to explain what had happened. The old man nodded as he set up the backgammon board. He and Shadow always had a game and Shadow always lost. Jimmy appeared again a few moments later looking his usual composed self.

"Have you fully recovered?" asked Shadow, trying not to smile.

"That dog is a monster! He never stopped pulling for a second. My arm feels like it's been stretched six inches," Jimmy complained, holding both arms in front of him to check their length.

"You make the poor thing sound like the Hound of the Baskervilles." Angela laughed, not even attempting to hide her amusement.

"You're wasting your time alluding to literature, Angela. I swear your brother is one of the worst-read people I have ever met. He hadn't even heard of *Hamlet* or *Lord of the Rings*."

"That's not fair, Chief," protested Jimmy. "I had heard of them, I just didn't get the reference straight away. I never saw the point of reading the book when it was quicker to watch the film." Shadow and Angela both tutted loudly and shook their heads, but Jimmy ignored their ribbing and continued, "Anyway, at school, I was always more into science than the arts."

"Then you went and broke Mum's heart by not becoming a doctor," teased Angela, who was training to become a teacher.

Shadow laughed. "Well, I can understand why she would be disappointed about him joining the police. Has she forgiven him yet?"

"Oh, Mum will forgive Jimmy anything. He'll always be the blue-eyed boy," replied Angela, who was, as usual, translating their conversation back to her grandfather, so he didn't feel left out.

The old man seemed to query what she was saying. Angela then turned to Shadow.

"Grandad was confused about what I said, so I explained that 'blue-eyed boy' is just a saying. I know Jimmy could only really have brown eyes like Mum and Dad."

"Ah, well, that's where you are wrong for once, sis," jumped in Jimmy, good-humouredly. "Two brown-eyed parents can have a blue-eyed child, but not the other way around. Two blues cannot make a brown. It's a genetic thing. You see I can remember some stuff from school."

"Very impressive," said Shadow with a smile.

"It would be if it wasn't out of date," retorted Angela. "It's been proven there are exceptions to that theory."

Jimmy rolled his eyes and held up his hands in mock surrender.

"Okay, Einstein! Whatever! My point is my brain is wired to remember scientific stuff and not that *Hamlet* was based on some prince in a Viking legend."

Jimmy's grandfather, who appeared to be listening intently, suddenly broke into a broad grin as he pointed to Shadow. "Viking!" he stated firmly. Angela and Jimmy both laughed.

"He thinks you're like a Viking with your blue eyes, Chief!"

Shadow smiled politely and nodded at Jimmy's grandfather. He was never sure how much English the old man understood. Up until now, the only words he'd heard him utter were *Win!* when he invariably beat Shadow at backgammon and *Elvis*. Apparently, he was a big fan of the singer. Growing up in Macau, the only western music he had heard was the casinos constantly playing "Viva Las Vegas".

CHAPTER NINE

Down 8 (6 letters)
I would hate to fail my relatives

LATER THAT EVENING, as he walked home, having eaten a mountain of beef in black bean sauce and being soundly beaten at backgammon yet again, Shadow thought about Jimmy's family. As an only child who merely had a few fleeting childhood memories of his father, he was always interested in the dynamics of other people's families.

Three generations of Jimmy's family lived under one roof, but it seemed to work well despite the occasional bout of bickering between the siblings. Jimmy's grandfather in particular seemed very content. The old man's ready smile and thatch of thick hair had been inherited by both his grandchildren. While Angela and her mother had the same beautiful almond-shaped eyes. Jimmy must have inherited his height from his father, whom Shadow had never met, but there was a photo of him hanging close to the kitchen.

If he and Luisa had been lucky enough to have children, he wondered what they would have looked like. Would they have her dark hair and wonderful brown eyes or his blue ones? He had been thinking about families a lot recently. When he was younger, his grandparents had often told him that he looked like his father, but as his mother hadn't been able to bear having any photographs of him on show, he'd been unable to judge properly for himself.

Suddenly, halfway across Skeldergate Bridge, he stopped in his tracks as a thought struck him. An image of Bjorn in the interview room with his dark, angry eyes flashing had sprung into his head. Edward's eyes behind those half-moon glasses were pale blue, and although Shadow had not studied the photo of Agnetha in detail, she had looked typically Scandinavian. Blonde hair and blue eyes. Which meant according to Jimmy's basic schoolroom science Bjorn was unlikely to be Edward's son. Agnetha had been having an affair with Alfred and she had died shortly after giving birth to Bjorn. Shadow thought of Bjorn's bullying, selfish nature. It might not only be eye colour Bjorn had inherited from his real father.

Shadow's thoughts veered back to the tale of Ragnar he had been reading. Hadn't he had a son with another woman? That son had been called Bjorn. Is that why Alfred had chosen the name King Ragnar for the Viking Festival? It couldn't be a coincidence surely?

Although he was almost home, Shadow turned and quickly headed back to the station. It was after nine o'clock at night when he arrived. He was surprised to find George was still working.

"Everything all right down there?" Shadow asked, nodding towards the steps leading down to the custody suite.

"Well, we've had quieter guests. Bennington has only just shut up. He's spent the last two hours shouting about police brutality."

"What brutality?" Shadow asked, looking shocked. It wasn't an accusation that had ever been levelled at his officers before.

"He's blaming us because he scalded his hand when he threw that cup of coffee at the wall. But it's nothing – I put some ointment on it."

Shadow shook his head at the thought of George playing nursemaid. So much for Bjorn being a tough guy.

"You're working late, aren't you?" he asked.

"You and me both by the look of things," agreed George. "I'm not going to be popular at home. I promised Carol I would start taking things a bit easier."

"Speaking of Carol, did either of you know Agnetha, Edward Bennington's wife and Bjorn's mother? She died about twenty-five years ago, around the same time Alfred discovered the Fulford Hoard?"

George's forehead creased into deep furrows as he thought back. "Yes, I do remember. Agnetha, very pretty, long blonde hair. I seem to remember everyone was quite amazed when Edward Bennington returned from Norway with her. Carol wasn't her friend exactly, but they did know each other. Years ago, Carol was a secretary here at the station. Do you remember she used to help out on the central emergency switchboard when we had one?"

Shadow shook his head. It was before his time.

George carried on. "Anyway, at the same time, Agnetha worked in admin over at the coroner's office, so they often had to phone each other. Well, you know Carol, she'll chat away to anyone given half a chance. The woman could talk the hind leg off a donkey. So, they got to know each other quite well. I remember Carol was upset when she heard about Agnetha's death. She collapsed at work not long before her baby was due. It's a real shame to think that baby has ended up here in our cells."

"Was it common knowledge that she was having an affair with Alfred Campbell?"

George looked surprised and shook his head. "Not as far as I know. I do recall Carol being a bit shocked about something one of the ambulance drivers told her. They said Agnetha had taken something. I can't remember whether it was drink or pills, but I know Carol was shocked. She always said Agnetha was a bit of a hippy, very clean living, didn't drink, was into herbal remedies – that type."

Shadow scratched his head and frowned as he considered what George had said. He didn't even know Agnetha had worked in the coroner's office. None of this new information had been in the report about her death or Sophie would have mentioned it. Did Astrid know? If she did, that was another reason for her to be keen to speak with Plunkett.

"It doesn't make any sense," he said almost to himself.

His old friend patted Shadow on the back and yawned as he made his way back down the stairs. "Never said it did, John," he replied.

SHADOW TRUDGED UPSTAIRS still trying to process everything he'd recently learnt. Although there were still a few constables wandering the corridors, the incident room felt eerily quiet without the constant chatter and ringing phones. The cold white glow from the new light bulbs did nothing to improve the atmosphere.

He leaned against a desk and surveyed the large whiteboard that took up most of one wall. He stared at all the photos stuck up there. As he looked at Bjorn and Alfred more closely, he was amazed he had never noticed the resemblance before. So now it seemed Alfred had three sons and Edward had no natural children of his own. Did he know? Did anyone? If Plunkett knew that Bjorn was Alfred's son, perhaps he thought he might have more use than just as someone to do his dirty work.

If only there was a photo up there of Agnetha too. She may be long gone, but now he had the feeling she was also involved in the case somehow. Astrid obviously thought there was something strange about her mother's death. And what was the connection with her working in the coroner's office? Was it possible Agnetha discovered Plunkett had kept some of the Viking treasure? Did Alfred know about it?

His jumbled thoughts were disturbed by the sound of heavy feet running down the corridor. He looked up as Tom appeared, flushed with excitement in the doorway.

"Chief Inspector Shadow, sorry to disturb you, sir, but we've got a report of an armed break-in at the Daneholm Viking museum on Coppergate," he announced breathlessly.

Shadow stood up in surprise. An armed incident of any sort in York was extremely rare. That it was happening at Alfred's museum was surely too much of a coincidence.

"All right, thank you, Constable. Can you inform Sergeant Chang?" Shadow asked as he zipped up his coat.

"He's already there, sir. He was the first on the scene and put the call out. I could drive you down there if you like, sir," Tom offered eagerly.

"No, no, I'll get there quick enough on foot," replied Shadow as he strode out of the incident room. He'd had more than enough of being in cars with young men who thought they were racing drivers for one day.

Shadow hurried through the empty streets towards Coppergate. The night air was cool and damp, and a mist was beginning to settle over the city. As he approached Coppergate, through the gloom he could see the outline of the museum. It was all in darkness, but the building's alarm was ringing loudly. He was surprised to find both the bar, Asgard, and Valhalla nightclub also in darkness.

There was a note on the door of the bar to say they were closed out of respect. Shadow turned his head suddenly at another sound. It was an approaching siren. He prayed an ambulance wasn't needed already, but as the vehicle swung around the corner with its flashing blue lights, he saw it was the van of the armed response unit. The fact that they had been called out was worrying enough. Shadow waited for them to screech to a halt and several officers jumped out in full protective uniform. He held up his hands to them.

"Hold on a second, lads," he said. "I want to go in and find out what we are dealing with."

The members of the armed response unit exchanged worried glances.

"It is procedure for us to go in first, sir," said the sergeant as he raised his visor.

"I understand, but my colleague is in there. I don't want us to do anything that could put him in danger."

The armed officers agreed to wait outside until they were called. They could hardly argue as Shadow outranked them.

The chief inspector gently pushed open the door and stepped inside. It was dark except for an eerie green glow from the lights on the security signs. He quickly put his hand over his nose as the museum's all too authentic smell suddenly hit him. As he slowly walked forward, he could just make out the shape of Jimmy standing on the edge of the Viking village.

"What's the situation?" he asked Jimmy, who was looking uncharacteristically anxious.

"It's Edward Bennington, Chief," Jimmy replied, struggling to make himself heard above the piercing noise of the alarm. "He's a director here, so he's got keys. He let himself in but managed to set the alarm off, panicked, and now he's barricaded himself in the tanner's hut."

"I was told it was an armed break-in," said Shadow. "There are three officers with guns outside."

"Well, he's armed now, Chief. He got hold of the Ulfberht sword. The original of the copy that was stuck in Alfred."

Shadow recalled how fascinated Edward had been with the replica sword on the night they discovered Alfred. "Do you think he's violent? Has he threatened you?" asked Shadow, although he found it hard to imagine the mild-mannered, slightly dull man ever being aggressive unless he'd finally found his inner Viking.

Jimmy shook his head. "No, Chief, nothing like that, but I am worried that he'll try to injure himself. I tried approaching him, but he was sobbing his heart out, so I backed off again. I didn't want to make the situation worse."

"I'll go and talk to him. You see if you can find out how to turn that damn alarm off," said Shadow. He slowly began moving towards the tanner's hut. Walking through the replica village was unsettling. With the low lighting, the mannequins dressed in their Viking clothing looked incredibly lifelike. Suddenly there was silence. The alarm had stopped. Shadow gave his head a shake. His ears were still ringing.

"Mr Bennington?" he called softly. "Edward? It's Chief Inspector Shadow here." He paused and listened. There were some audible snuffing sounds coming from inside the hut. Shadow gave a sigh of relief. Like Jimmy, he had been concerned Edward wanted to seriously harm himself. At least he knew he was still conscious. He edged closer.

Although Shadow found the whole place quite creepy, perhaps this was Edward's idea of heaven. That's why he had come here. Finally, he was among the people he had studied for so long, even if they weren't real.

Shadow carefully stepped over a low wooden fence into the tanner's yard. He manoeuvred his way around the precisely arranged barrels, fake pieces of leather draped on rails, and the cheerful-looking tanner himself, holding some sort of scraping implement. The hut was made of wood with fake turf covering the roof. A red piece of cloth hung down, covering the doorway. Someone, Shadow assumed Edward, had dragged two large wooden troughs across the entrance too. Slightly to the left of the doorway was a narrow opening for a window. Shadow got as close to the hut as he dared and tried peering through the window, but it was so dark inside he could barely make anything out.

"Edward?" he called out again. "Can you hear me?"

There was the sound of more sniffing and then a small, frightened voice finally responded.

"I'm very sorry, Chief Inspector," he whispered.

"That's all right, Edward," replied Shadow calmly. "Everything is going to be fine. Are you hurt at all?"

"I'm sorry," Edward repeated. "I simply couldn't bear to see it all go, you see. All this – it's been my life's work. If it goes it will all have been for nothing. I couldn't bear it." His voice cracked and the sobbing started again. Shadow didn't know what he was talking about; he just wanted to be sure he hadn't injured himself in any way. He certainly sounded desperate enough.

All of a sudden, there was a loud clatter, as the three members of the armed response unit came crashing through the door.

"Tell them to stay back," hissed Shadow angrily. Jimmy sprinted over to the officers to pass on the instruction and usher them back outside.

"I'm going to be in an awful lot of trouble, aren't I, Chief Inspector?" asked the frail voice from inside the hut.

"You need to come out of there now, Edward," Shadow insisted gently. "The quicker this is all over the better for everyone."

All of a sudden, there was another loud bang, this time on the other side of the village.

"For crying out loud!" Shadow groaned under his breath. In exasperation, he looked round to see Dan and Astrid coming through what he supposed must be the back door. Jimmy rushed over to them and from his gestures, Shadow could see he was explaining the situation.

"Dad, please stop this. Please come out," called Astrid.

"Edward, don't be stupid. You can have the sword. Just come out now," Dan added.

Then Jimmy bent down and hurried over to Shadow so Edward wouldn't see him, while Astrid and Dan waited with their arms around each other, looking nervous. Jimmy crouched next to Shadow, who frowned at his sergeant.

"Those two shouldn't be in here," he whispered.

"I know, Chief," whispered back Jimmy, "but Dan was called out by the alarm company because he's a key holder. Astrid was with him and when the guys outside told them what was going on, they wanted to try and help. It seems Edward overheard Dan talking about selling the museum and the bar and, well, he had a bit of a meltdown."

"That's putting it mildly," said Shadow. He recalled Dan saying he wanted to get rid of everything when they had spoken in the bar. He turned back to the window.

"Did you hear that, Edward? Astrid and Dan are both here. They are very worried about you."

"I really didn't want to cause anyone any trouble. I'm so sorry," sniffed Edward.

"We know that, Edward. We understand. We can end all this now. Is that what you want?"

"Yes, please," came the almost inaudible reply.

"Good," said Shadow, feeling very relieved that Edward was listening to reason. He glanced over to where Dan and

Astrid were standing behind them. He gave them a silent thumbs-up sign, then turned back to the window. "Now, when you are ready, Edward, come to the door, nice and slowly and so we can see the sword."

Jimmy began to slowly push the two wooden troughs away from the doorway. Shadow carefully pulled back the red piece of cloth hanging down and tied it to one side. Then very slowly Edward appeared at the entrance. He looked small and fragile and his glasses were crooked on his nose. His arms were raised above his head. In one hand he held a damp white handkerchief and in the other was the Ulfberht sword. It hardly looked worth stealing with its worn-away handle and jagged, rusting-away blade.

"That's it," encouraged Shadow, keeping his voice low and even, "nice and steady, Edward."

Shadow and Jimmy both stood very still with their arms by their sides as Edward shuffled closer towards them.

"Well done, Dad," called Astrid. Edward looked up and smiled weakly as a tear trickled down his face.

"Now, when you are ready, place the sword on the floor," Shadow continued. "In your own time, Edward."

Very slowly, Edward bent his knees and lowered his arm holding the sword. Then, just as he was about to place the ancient weapon on the ground, he stumbled and fell. Jimmy stepped forward to help him, but as he did so, the tip of the sword pierced Jimmy's trainers and went straight into the sergeant's foot. Jimmy cried out in pain. Then chaos.

Astrid and Dan ran towards Edward. Shadow ran to help Jimmy and the armed response team burst in with their weapons raised and started shouting at everyone to "Get down!" Shadow quickly grabbed the sword and stood in the middle of all the mayhem with his hands raised.

"Everybody, calm down," he ordered and turned to the armed unit. "Thank you for attending, officers, but the situation is now under control. You can stand down."

The officers lowered their guns and stepped back. Shadow switched his attention to Jimmy and Edward.

Jimmy had removed his trainer and was clutching his foot. It was bleeding profusely, and he looked very pale. Edward meanwhile was sobbing loudly as Astrid cradled him in her arms. They clearly both need hospital treatment and as soon as possible. Shadow recalled the large armoured van with flashing lights waiting outside.

"Is there room for us all in the van?" he asked, turning towards the armed sergeant.

"Yes, sir," was the immediate response from the visor-wearing sergeant.

"Is Dad under arrest?" asked Astrid.

"I don't want to press charges," Dan added immediately.

"Not right now," replied Shadow. He was no doctor, but in his eyes, Edward was in no fit state to answer any questions. He needed to be in a ward, not in a cell. Dan and Astrid assisted Edward into the rear of the van, while the two armed constables helped Jimmy.

AFTER AN EXTREMELY fast but uncomfortable ride with Edward sobbing and Jimmy groaning, but at the same time insisting he was fine, they all arrived at the hospital. One of the armed officers had radioed ahead and there was a trolley waiting to take Edward inside. Dan and Astrid hurried after him. Jimmy leant heavily on Shadow as he half hopped into the Accident and Emergency Department. A nurse came running forward with a wheelchair for him and Shadow stepped aside.

"I'll be back to see how you are doing in a few minutes," he said.

"Chief," Jimmy called after him, "make sure my mum doesn't find out. She'll only worry."

Shadow nodded in agreement. The last thing he needed tonight was having to deal with a hysterical Rose. He checked with the reception desk and discovered that Edward had been taken up to the psychiatric ward to be assessed. Shadow made his way up to the second floor and waited as he saw Dan and Astrid talking to one of the doctors. When they had finished their conversation, Astrid followed the doctor through to the ward while Dan, who had spotted Shadow, came over to speak with him.

"How is he?" Shadow asked.

"Sleeping, they gave him something to calm him down, and it seemed to knock him out, poor guy."

"I will still need to speak with him."

"I understand. A psychiatrist is meant to be assessing him in the morning. The doctor we just spoke to thinks he might have had some sort of breakdown. I guess with everything that's happened to him over the years it was inevitable. I'm only amazed it didn't happen sooner. If all is well tomorrow, we'll bring him to the station, okay?"

"Okay," agreed Shadow, although from what Dan had said, he doubted Edward would be up to it. "By the way, you have probably heard we arrested Martin Plunkett today. On the night Chloe and Alfred were killed, I saw you arguing with him. Was it about the terms of your annulment?"

"No, Chief Inspector. That was all done and dusted. Chloe said she had been forced into the marriage. That was a total lie – she couldn't wait to be married. It was a lie cooked up by Plunkett, but if it was the only way to be rid of her then, quite frankly, I would have agreed to anything."

"So, what was the argument about?" asked Shadow, feeling a little confused. Dan had told him he was in Chloe's tent to discuss the annulment, yet he had just admitted that matter was finished with. Had he forgotten what he had already said? Was he lying now or when they'd first met? Dan continued seemingly unaware he had said anything to confuse the detective.

"Astrid has been looking into her mother's death recently. Plunkett worked with Agnetha back then, but he refused to help Astrid. He wouldn't even return her calls, so when I saw him, I told him what I thought of him for ignoring her."

Shadow shook Dan's hand and wished him goodnight. Again, he was reminded of Astrid using the word *farce* to describe the situation around the annulment. He was beginning to agree with her.

Jimmy was also being kept in overnight for assessment, according to the emergency nurse Shadow spoke to. They were making him comfortable in his room. Shadow followed her instructions and went up to the fourth floor. He paused in the corridor and decided to take Jimmy a coffee. His sergeant seemed to live on little else so it might cheer him up.

He waited in front of the coffee machine as the hot brown liquid spluttered into two plastic cups. As he stood there a blonde young woman hurried past him. She looked so pale and agitated he almost didn't recognise her.

"Sophie?" he called out. She stopped and spun round.

"Oh, hello, Chief, is he okay?" she asked. Her voice was strained and urgent.

"He's fine – it's just a flesh wound," he reassured her. "They're keeping him in overnight, but only for observation. How did you know he was here?"

A look of relief swept over her face. "We'd arranged to meet for a drink after I'd finished at the university, but he sent me a text to say he was investigating a break-in at the Viking museum. I headed down there, but it was all in darkness when I arrived, so I called the station and they told me what happened."

Shadow had never seen her so upset. She was normally so calm, self-assured, and unflappable.

"That's his room, second on the left." He nodded down the corridor. Sophie smiled her thanks and hurried away.

Shadow returned to the coffee machine and retrieved the two cups. He also made his way down to Jimmy's room but paused outside the door. Through the small window he watched as Sophie talked intensely, sitting next to Jimmy's bed, and he took her hand as if to reassure her. Shadow had known they were seeing each other, but it felt strange to see for himself how close his two young colleagues had become.

"Do you want me to get the door for you, Chief Inspector?" asked a friendly nurse passing by. Shadow looked down at the cups of coffee in his hands.

"Oh, would you mind taking these in for me, nurse? I've been called away suddenly," he lied. He would feel like he was intruding if he went in there now.

HE WALKED DOWN the corridor and was relieved to see the lift door slide open as he approached. He stepped inside and nodded politely to the elderly couple already there. As they all began to descend, he noticed the couple were edging away from him and the lady had discreetly covered her nose. He raised his arm and sniffed his jacket, then instantly wished he hadn't. The museum staff were right – the scent of the Viking village certainly did linger.

Once on the ground floor, he walked through the still-busy hospital reception and out into the car park. It was now the early hours of the morning and the air was cold and damp. He turned up the collar of his jacket, pushed his hands into his pockets, and walked through the deserted streets back to *Florence*. Along Clarence Street he passed a board showing a copy of that evening's *Herald*. The headline read, "VIKING MURDERS – Mad Swordsman Still At Large – Police Make No Progress." Shadow sighed. Kevin MacNab clearly had not forgiven them for taking his disc.

The Minster bells were striking three when he finally returned to the riverbank. The geese honked angrily at him for waking them up.

"Oh, be quiet!" he grumbled. He stepped aboard *Florence* and headed straight for the bedroom. He kicked off his shoes, shrugged off his jacket, and flopped straight into bed with a heavy sigh. What a day! As he drifted off to sleep, his brain ran through all the reasons he had encountered throughout his career that led people to kill. Anger, jealousy, greed, revenge, fear. All these powerful emotions were present in this case, but which had fuelled the murders of Chloe and Alfred?

THE NEXT MORNING, after breakfast, Shadow returned to the hospital. His first port of call was the psychiatric ward. The sister in charge told him Edward had slept well.

"Do you think there's any chance he'll be up to answering a few questions later?" asked Shadow hopefully.

The sister arched an eyebrow and looked at Shadow as if he should know better. "No, Chief Inspector, not unless the questions you had in mind are: Would you like tea or coffee?" she replied briskly.

Shadow took the hint and turned to go. He would have liked to speak to Edward, but not about the break-in. Jimmy's injury was an accident and as Edward had keys to Daneholm and Dan would not press charges, the matter would be dropped. However, Shadow did want to ask him about Agnetha and everything that had happened all those years ago.

Shadow had a great deal of sympathy for Edward. He remembered him saying life was too short to bear a grudge, yet last night he had snapped and acted completely out of character. Shadow wondered if it was possible the same thing had happened on the night Chloe and Alfred were killed. After all he was the first person to discover Alfred's body.

JIMMY WAS SITTING up in bed looking much brighter than when Shadow had last seen him.

"How are you?" asked Shadow as he stepped into the room.

"Loads better thanks, Chief. I'll be fine. Last night they gave me four stitches and a tetanus jab. Sorry, Chief," he added, seeing Shadow already beginning to turn green. "The specialist checked me over a few minutes ago and there's no ligament damage, so I'll be discharged in the next hour or so."

"Excellent news. It looks like Edward Bennington will be staying in for a while yet." He went on to fill Jimmy in on everything, including the news that he believed Bjorn was Alfred's son.

"Then surely that gives all three Benningtons a motive, Chief. Last night we saw that it has all been too much for Edward. Astrid has been looking into her mother's death and maybe she blamed Alfred and killed him in revenge. Bjorn could have wanted revenge too or maybe he thought he would be due some inheritance. We know how greedy he is."

Similar thoughts had been going through Shadow's head. He was about to agree, but at that moment the door burst open to reveal a distraught-looking Rose.

"Oh, my poor baby!" she cried as she hurried over to her son's bedside, then stopped in her tracks when she saw the dressing on his arm. "They said it was your foot. What happened to your arm?"

Jimmy was squirming in embarrassment as Rose fussed over him.

"Don't worry, Mum, that's only a tattoo," he explained with a slight cringe.

Rose gasped in horror, then turned angrily to Shadow. "Chief Inspector! What were you thinking? How could you let him get injured and get a tattoo?"

Shadow mumbled an apology as he quickly backed out of the room. He hurriedly walked down the corridor and could still hear Rose's voice swinging between berating and consoling as Jimmy tried to calm her down. He pressed the button for the lift and waited.

A few seconds later, the doors slid open to reveal two orderlies with a trolley holding an unconscious patient hooked up to all manner of tubes and drips. Shadow quickly stepped back and waved an apology. There was no way he could be in a confined space with all that. Instead he turned around and pushed open the heavy doors that led to the central stairwell.

With a deep sigh, he began the four-flight descent he had managed to avoid the night before. Halfway down he paused on one of the landings to catch his breath. A visit to the hospital always made him feel lightheaded, but the lack of sleep and heavy breakfast he had consumed before coming certainly weren't helping. He rummaged in his pocket for a couple of indigestion tablets and popped them in his mouth.

As he waited for them to dissolve, he stared out of the window. The hospital was built in a U-shape with a large car park and ambulance bay in the middle. A small familiar figure with long grey hair caught his eye. She had emerged from the building opposite him. Annabel was alone. Shadow watched as she pulled on her coat. She looked quite composed. Shadow wondered if she had been to visit Edward. Although his stomach was still churning, he continued descending the stairs and stepped outside.

He took several deep breaths of fresh air to clear the hospital smell from his nostrils. Annabel was now nowhere to be seen. He looked across the car park to the door she had stepped out of. The name above stated it was the Marigold Wing. It didn't necessarily follow that Annabel herself was ill. She could quite easily have been visiting a friend. Shadow paused for a few seconds, wondering if he should go inside, but reasoned that even if Annabel was a patient there, they would not release her medical records to him. With a sigh, he set off on the long walk from the hospital to Micklegate.

His walk home from the Golden Dragon last night and its revelations seemed like a long time ago, but there were still some loose ends he needed to tie up about Bjorn and his paternity. There was also something that had been bothering him since his first conversation with Martin Plunkett. He hoped Cornelius Rutherford would be able to help him with both.

RUTHERFORDS' SOLICITORS HAD their offices in a tall thin

Victorian red-brick building on Micklegate. There was a discreet gleaming brass plate on the oak front door that stated they had been practising there since 1896. Cornelius Rutherford was the fourth generation of his family to be a lawyer and was almost a city icon. As short as he was wide and always dressed in tweed with a bow tie, he could always be seen puffing up and down the steep cobbles of Micklegate.

Shadow stepped inside and waved to the receptionist, who was busily watering the many plants on her desk. He trudged up the creaking stairs to Rutherford's office on the first floor. His secretary recognised Shadow immediately and greeted him with a bright smile.

"Good morning, Chief Inspector, I hope you are well. Now, go right on in. He's drafting a will, so he'll welcome the distraction."

Shadow did as she said, but briefly knocked on the heavy oak door before turning the handle. He stepped into the solicitor's office with its book-lined walls and faint smell of furniture polish. Rutherford raised his head and peered at Shadow over his steel-rimmed glasses.

"Good grief! None of my clients have died, have they?"

"Not that I'm aware of." Shadow smiled. He had always admired the solicitor's directness. Many would say it was an attribute the two men shared.

"Well, that's a relief. You do have a touch of the grim reaper about you, Shadow." It was true. The two men only really crossed paths when Shadow had an interest in one of Rutherford's recently departed clients. Rutherford stood up and reached across to shake the chief inspector's hand and motioned for him to sit down in the slightly worn leather chair opposite him.

"I wanted to ask you about Annabel Campbell," began Shadow. "I understand she recently tried to arrange a meeting with Alfred, her ex-husband, about their divorce settlement. Can you give me any more details?"

"Don't be ridiculous." Rutherford laughed good-naturedly. "You know perfectly well I can't break client confidentiality without Annabel's permission, which I presume you don't have."

"No," sighed Shadow, "but I thought it was worth a try. How about a hypothetical question?"

"Go ahead," agreed the solicitor.

"If during a divorce, one parent got full custody of any children from the marriage, and if that parent then died, what would happen to any children involved?"

Rutherford did not hesitate. "Custody would go to the surviving parent. The court would view any custody case ended on the death of the other parent." He paused for a second. "Hypothetically, of course."

Shadow nodded. That solved one conundrum.

"Anything else?" asked Rutherford.

Shadow remembered the other reason for his visit. "Yes. Would an illegitimate child automatically inherit from their parent?"

"Good God, no! We're not French!" exclaimed the solicitor in horror. "They would have to contest the will like anyone else."

Shadow smiled. Their neighbours across the Channel often had a more pragmatic way of dealing with infidelity and its results.

"By the way," continued Rutherford, "I hear you had a spot of bother with Astrid's father last night."

"That's right." Shadow nodded. "But nothing will come of it. We won't be pressing charges."

"I'm pleased to hear it, for your sake as well as Edward's. Astrid's best friend is Grace Patel. She's a barrister down in London, quite the rising star I hear. No doubt Astrid would have asked her to represent Edward and made mincemeat out of you all in court."

"Thanks for the warning," said Shadow, standing up to leave. "Do I take it Miss Patel's services won't be called upon to assist Bjorn?"

"No." Rutherford chuckled. "With him you can throw away the key. On that subject, how is our esteemed city councillor and my fellow lawyer? Has he managed to wriggle his way out of his cell yet?"

"I think I can safely say Mr Plunkett won't be wriggling anywhere for a while," said Shadow as he shook the solicitor's hand once more. He waved goodbye to the secretary and receptionist on the way out and stepped through the heavy outer oak door of Rutherford's offices and into Micklegate.

As he did so, he almost bumped into Dan, who was on his way in.

"Good morning, Chief Inspector. How's Sergeant Chang?" he asked politely.

"He'll live," said Shadow. "Edward is staying in hospital, though, I understand."

"Yes. I am sorry he won't be able to speak to you. The doctor said he needs complete rest, at least for a few days." Dan sounded genuinely apologetic. "We are going to see him now. Astrid had a meeting first thing this morning, so I said I would meet her here and then take her up to the hospital."

"That was kind of you. The two of you seem to be close."

Shadow watched as for the first time Dan's face broke into a broad smile instead of his usual brooding expression. He looked totally transformed.

"Astrid is great," he enthused. "We've known each other for years, but I must have been an idiot not to see it before. She's fantastic with Will too. One of her clients is president of an animal welfare charity and she's got him a job helping out there. He'll absolutely love it."

"That's good news. I'm very pleased for him and you." Shadow paused, not quite sure how to broach the next subject. "While I was at the hospital," he began, "I also happened to see your mother leaving the Marigold Wing."

The two men looked each other in the eye for a moment and Dan's smile faded. Shadow knew then that Annabel wasn't visiting a friend, but had an appointment herself in that part of the hospital. Despite its pretty name, it was in fact the cancer treatment centre.

"Yes, she beat it once a couple of years ago, but it came back. Now she goes to the hospital every couple of weeks, even though there isn't much they can do anymore. Afterwards she always goes to Rowntree Park to feed the ducks and cheer herself up," Dan explained, his voice faltering slightly.

"You don't go with her to the appointments?" asked Shadow.

"No, I've offered, but she prefers to go alone. She thinks it will upset me." He shook his head as he spoke. "Her whole life she has put Will and me first."

When he uttered this last sentence, he sounded almost angry, as if Shadow had suggested his mother had not always done her best for her sons. Shadow compared the way Dan looked and sounded when he spoke about Annabel to the emotionless way he had discussed Alfred's death when they had first met. He patted the young man on the shoulder and wished him goodbye.

All at once, Annabel's tired appearance and her rather frantic cooking to fill the freezer began to make sense. Shadow realised with a jolt that having already lost their father, Dan and Will may soon become orphans. He was overwhelmed with a feeling of sadness. Hadn't that family been through enough?

Shadow plodded down the gently sloping street towards Ouse Bridge. He was tempted to head back to *Florence* for a little while. Perhaps he could manage a half-hour nap before returning to the station to interview Plunkett and Bjorn again.

It was a warm day for the time of year and the sun was shining on the river. A group of music students were busking at the top of the steps down to the river. They were playing popular songs from films and had just delighted a group of visiting school children with a rendition of "The Bare Necessities". They were now playing a song from *Oliver!* Shadow wasn't a great fan of musicals, but his mother had loved them.

He remembered watching the film of *Oliver!* when he was a child. Bull's-eye, Bill Sikes's loyal dog, had always been his favourite, but his mother had liked Nancy best. She would try singing her songs, but never very successfully. Shadow found himself humming along with the band now, "Oom pah pah," as he took the steps down to the path by the river.

Suddenly he froze. A chill ran down his spine. When his mother sang, it sounded wrong not only because she couldn't carry a tune but because her voice was unmistakably north-ern. Everything was beginning to make sense. A breeze from the river blew a few leaves off the branches of the tree in front of him. As he watched each float to the ground it was as though a part of the case was falling into place. Will's cat. The am-dram society. The two phones. His conversations with Julie and Rutherford. He felt like kicking himself. Last night when he had considered what led people to kill, he'd forgotten the most powerful emotion of all. Love.

CHAPTER TEN

Across 9 (6 letters)
A maternal figure Tom meets her

S HADOW TOOK A second to collect himself, then continued down the steps and along the path by the river.
Rowntree Park was not very far from where *Florence* was
moored. It was a twenty-acre park given to the city in order
to commemorate those who had worked in the famous
Rowntree chocolate factory and lost their lives during the
two world wars. It had been enjoyed by York families for
generations. There was a lake, tennis courts, a café, a bowling
green, and a children's playground. Recently, they had even
added a skate park.

Today, though, it was quiet. A couple of young mothers
strolled along chatting as their little children ran squealing in
excitement through the piles of fallen leaves. Shadow spotted
Annabel almost immediately. She was standing on the bridge
over the lake, throwing bread to the ducks quacking loudly
below. She looked so serene, Shadow felt guilty about
disturbing her. He walked slowly to join her on the bridge.
She turned when she heard his footsteps and gave him the

same bright smile he'd seen when they'd first met.

"Hello, Chief Inspector," she said, "I see you've found me, or should that be found me out?" She put her hand inside the carrier bag and gave a large chunk of bread to Shadow. "I used to bring the boys here when they were little," she continued. "They used to love it, especially Will. You know, I read somewhere that you shouldn't feed ducks bread, that lettuce is better for them, but they do seem to love this bread."

Shadow didn't say anything, but he was relieved Annabel sounded as accepting of the situation as she had been about Will and the blue rabbit. He tore off several pieces of bread and threw them out into the lake. The ducks noisily swarmed after them.

"What gave me away?" Annabel asked calmly.

"It was something Edward Bennington said when I saw you both in the bar," replied Shadow.

"Good heavens!" Annabel smiled. "You must be one of the only people to ever pay close attention to what Edward says. Poor old thing! It sounds like everything got a little too much for him last night, but Astrid tells me he'll be fine."

"Yes, I called in at the hospital this morning to see how he was. I also saw you leaving your appointment."

"Oh, I see." She threw another piece of bread to the quacking ducks.

"Can I ask how long the doctors have given you?"

"A few weeks, maybe a couple of months if I'm lucky."

They stood together in silence for a few moments, simply feeding the greedy birds. Annabel put one foot on the lower rail of the bridge to raise herself up a little so she could throw the last of the bread to the shy moorhens behind the pushy ducks. Shadow instinctively put a hand out to stop her.

"Don't worry, Chief Inspector." She laughed. "I'm not planning on doing anything silly. Your arrival isn't a total shock. I always knew I couldn't possibly get away with it and in some ways, I didn't want to. I knew you would find me out. You see it all happened on the spur of the moment – you may not believe me, but it really did. Do you already know everything?"

"I think I've worked most of it out, but I'd still like to hear the truth from you."

"Very well, Chief Inspector, then I shall start at the beginning," she said, sounding as if she was about to tell him a bedtime story. "It was after Alfred and the Great Heathen Army had marched off and left St Sampson's Square. Most of the tents were closing as the tourists went to watch the longboat race. I saw Dan go into Chloe's tent and watched their silhouettes as they argued inside."

"But their marriage was already annulled, so they weren't arguing about that – like Dan first told me."

"No, Chief Inspector, Dan said that to try and put you off the scent, but as I said our plan wasn't very well thought through. Dan had really gone to plead with Chloe to try and help change Alfred's mind about claiming custody of Will.

Do you know all about that?"

Shadow nodded his head to acknowledge he did, and Annabel gave a heavy sigh.

"When the doctors told me there was nothing more they could do, I tried to talk to Alfred. To reason with him, beg him even. Dan was more than happy to become Will's guardian, but Alfred was adamant custody should go to him and for no other reason than his need for control and his cruelty. He would have put Will in some institution. Taken him away from his brother, his animals, everything he loves." Annabel's voice caught in her throat.

She took a deep breath and composed herself, before she continued, "Anyway, where was I? Oh yes, Chloe refused to help or say anything that might rock the boat with Alfred. I don't think she felt very secure in their relationship. She accused Dan of being jealous and interfering. She tried to storm off but slipped and fell in those silly shoes of hers. She banged her head on the iron candleholder. I ran into her tent to help. Dan wanted to call an ambulance, but I knew straight away she was dead." She suddenly turned to Shadow and looked very fierce despite her frailty. "I swear Dan didn't lay a finger on her, but I knew how it might look especially with their history. I didn't want Dan to be blamed, so I told him to leave. Of course, he didn't want to, but I made him go to the boat race, so as many people would see him as possible and hopefully give him an alibi.

"Then as I stood there looking down at Chloe, I thought

why should either of us be blamed? We'd all been through such a lot. That's when I had the thought that although it was an accident, I might be able to make it look like Alfred had killed Chloe. I tried to arrange her so she looked at rest, peaceful, closing her eyes and so forth, but I'm afraid I did tie the cord round her neck.

"Then I took her bag with me down to St George's Field. I thought I would…what's the word? Plant her bag amongst his things. On my way, her phone beeped and I saw a message from Alfred to meet him at Ragnar's Palace. He mentioned wearing a blindfold." She frowned and shook her head. "That's when I realised I might finally have the chance to get rid of that dreadful man from our lives forever. So, I texted back a suitable response, from Chloe's phone, as if it had been sent by her."

"Then you went to Ragnar's Palace and pretended to be Chloe by spraying her perfume around and mimicking her voice."

Annabel nodded her head and brushed a few stray hairs away from her face.

"Alfred was never a very bright man, and he was so conceited. Chloe always wore a bucketful of scent and had a very distinctive voice. So, when I knew he was alone in there, wearing the blindfold, I used the perfume and put on her voice so he wouldn't get suspicious. I told him he was about to get a surprise."

"And you killed him."

Annabel closed her eyes and nodded again. "His sword was just lying on the floor and he was in his chair with a big smile on his face. I would never have believed I was capable of killing someone, Chief Inspector, but all I could think about was how he wanted to have Will locked away. It made me so angry. I think that's what gave me the strength."

Despite the warmth from the sun, she shivered as she spoke.

"Come on, let's get you inside," Shadow suggested. She took his arm and he led her to the park's reading café. It was a tiny lending library that also served teas. They took a seat at one of the tables with blue-and-white-checked tablecloths and a waitress brought them a pot of tea for two almost immediately. Annabel poured them each a cup before she continued.

"Afterwards, I began to panic about the phone and bag. I had been careful with the sword, but I realised they would probably be covered in my fingerprints. Alfred's phone was on the table and I grabbed that too."

"So, you smashed both phones, put them in the bag, and dumped the bag in the Foss," said Shadow.

Annabel nodded. "Yes, I was quite jittery by then. I passed the Merchant Adventurers' Hall on my way home, but there was a party going on. I thought someone might see me, so I flung the bag in from the steps near the river."

Shadow nodded as he recalled Donaldson had been there at his Saltire Society Ball.

"And Dan knew all about this and agreed to cover for you?"

The fierceness returned to her eyes.

"It was all my idea. He knew nothing about it until afterwards and I'll swear to that in court, Chief Inspector. All he did was try to protect Will and me. We agreed what we would say when you arrived, but Dan, bless him, has never been able to lie convincingly. I tried to sound as confident and relaxed as I could for their sakes."

Shadow nodded. Her words echoed those Dan had spoken less than an hour ago about her. They sat in silence for a few minutes, sipping their tea.

"Can I ask you about Agnetha?" enquired Shadow cautiously. He was unsure how Annabel would react to discussing the woman her husband had been unfaithful with, but she merely smiled.

"Oh yes, poor Agnetha, such a beauty and a really good person. She was truly torn. She was very fond of Edward and grateful to him for giving her and Astrid a home, but then she fell in love with Alfred. Actually, she brought out the best in him. I think it was losing her that made Alfred behave the way he did. Don't get me wrong, Chief Inspector, he was always a selfish so-and-so, but Agnetha was the only person he ever really loved. It broke his heart when she left him. Of course, the pair of them had already broken Edward's heart."

"But not yours?" enquired Shadow gently.

Annabel shook her head. "No, I had fallen out of love

with Alfred long before he and Agnetha got together. Afterwards, he and I tried to patch things up for the sake of Dan and eventually Will came along, but we both knew our marriage was over. Alfred's reaction to Will's difficulties was the final straw for me."

"You said Agnetha left Alfred. They had split up before she died?"

"Yes, I'm not sure why. I would guess Agnetha realised as much as she loved Alfred, he wasn't going to be anything like the father Edward was to Astrid and she loved her little girl."

"What about Bjorn? Did Alfred know he was his son? Did you and Edward?"

"I suspected it, but I never discussed it directly with either of them. As far as Edward was concerned, Bjorn was his, but as the years went by how could anyone not know? Bjorn is so like Alfred in every way. Far more so than either Will or Dan."

"But Alfred never acknowledged him or made any provision for him?"

Annabel gave a firm shake of her head. "No, as I said, he adored Agnetha, but that love didn't extend to her children. The idea of having to share Agnetha's love with anyone would have been completely alien to him. He would probably even have been jealous of Astrid and Bjorn had Agnetha lived."

Shadow gave a deep sigh as he tried to fathom the complex relationships he was dealing with. "We have been looking into Agnetha's death recently," he said. "There seems to be a few discrepancies from what was reported at the inquest."

Annabel's brow furrowed. "That's what Astrid thinks too. The poor girl was just a tot when she lost her mother. It was a tragedy, Chief Inspector. I didn't go to the inquest, in fact I was minding Astrid for Edward, but you are quite right, what I heard reported about the whisky didn't seem to ring true. Unfortunately, at the time, Edward was too upset to do anything about it and Alfred had taken himself off to Guernsey when Agnetha ended their relationship."

They sat in silence for a few minutes as they finished their tea.

"You know we'll have to go to the station, and I will have to charge you?" said Shadow finally.

"Don't worry, I'll come quietly." Annabel smiled. "Isn't that what they say in the films, Chief Inspector?"

Shadow returned her smile and excused himself. He stepped outside, took his phone out of his pocket, and dialled the number for the station's front desk. He was surprised when Jimmy's voice answered.

"What are you doing there?" he asked without preamble.

"I'm just covering the desk, Chief. Bjorn is kicking off downstairs again, so Tom went to help George."

"No, I mean why aren't you resting at home?" asked Shadow, trying his hardest not to sound impatient with his sergeant so soon after he'd returned to work.

"Oh, I couldn't stay there, Chief. Mum was doing my head in, fussing over me all the time," he explained. "I'm fine. I've just got a bit of a limp."

"Good, well, in that case send a car to Rowntree Park for Annabel Campbell and me, will you?"

"Annabel?" Jimmy repeated in surprise.

"I'll explain everything later, but I think it's safe to say our murder investigation is over." He paused before he hung up. "Oh and, Jimmy, no lights or sirens, okay?"

Shadow slipped his phone back in his pocket and returned to the table where Annabel was waiting.

"I'll have a word with the Crown Prosecution Service and if necessary, the judge," he said. "Under the circumstances, I can't see any reason why you can't be charged then released on bail until the trial."

Annabel nodded gratefully. Neither of them said what Shadow imagined they were both thinking – that it was unlikely she would still be here to stand trial.

"Thank you, Chief Inspector, you're a very kind man," she said. "I am sorry to have wasted so much of your time. Please believe me when I say I would never have let anyone else take the blame. I know I should have confessed straightaway, but I thought I might be locked away. I only wanted to buy a little more time, a few extra days or perhaps weeks with my boys. There is so much I still wanted to do for them. Sadly you were too good at your job."

They stood up and Annabel stumbled slightly. Shadow

reached out a hand to steady her as they stepped outside. It was beginning to grow dark and the glow from the setting sun was reflected across the calm surface of the lake. A few moments later, Jimmy arrived as agreed in an unmarked car. Annabel took Shadow's arm as he walked her over and helped her into the back seat.

"Sorry for the delay, Chief," apologised Jimmy. "I had to find an automatic car because of the foot."

"How are you feeling now, Sergeant Chang?" enquired Annabel pleasantly.

"Oh, much better, thank you, Mrs Campbell," replied Jimmy politely.

Shadow twisted round in the passenger seat. "I am required to read you your rights," he explained.

Annabel leaned back and closed her eyes. "That's fine, Chief Inspector. You go right ahead," she said with a soft sigh.

As they drove towards the station, Shadow reflected that it was possibly the most dignified arrest he had ever made.

SHADOW AND JIMMY escorted Annabel down to the custody suite to find what appeared to be a welcoming committee waiting for them. Astrid, Dan, Will, and even Sophie was there chatting to George.

"I called Dan when you left the café, Chief Inspector,"

admitted Annabel. Shadow was not surprised. He had guessed as much.

As soon as Dan saw Annabel he stepped forward and enveloped his mother in a huge hug.

"Don't worry, Mum, everything is going to be okay," he reassured her. Shadow then noticed a petite dark-haired woman standing quietly beside Astrid. Judging by her well-cut black suit and the blue brief bag she was carrying, Shadow deduced she must be the criminal barrister from London, whom Rutherford had mentioned. Astrid followed the chief inspector's gaze.

"May I introduce, Grace Patel, Chief Inspector. She'll be acting for Annabel," Astrid explained.

Shadow nodded. He had been right. He shook the barrister's outstretched hand. "It's good to meet you, Miss Patel."

"Thank you, Chief Inspector. I'd like to speak with my client, if I may?"

Annabel reached up and gave Will a kiss on the cheek. The young man was clutching the old teddy bear Shadow had first seen him with. Shadow didn't want him to see his mother being charged, so he turned to Sophie.

"Would you mind taking Will upstairs?" he asked her.

"Sure," she replied and held out her hand. "Come on, Will, let's go and see if there's anything to eat in the station canteen and you can tell me all about the peregrine falcon you have been watching."

Will meekly took her hand as she led him away. Astrid and Dan each placed a hand on Annabel's shoulder as Shadow read out the charges. Grace then whisked her away into one of the interview rooms.

"She got here quickly," observed Shadow.

Astrid shrugged. "King's Cross is only two hours away, Chief Inspector. Besides Grace was on standby."

"When I saw you this morning, I guessed we were on borrowed time," added Dan. "I have never been much good at lying. I tried, but I know I kept slipping up."

Astrid quickly put a hand on his arm to silence him before he incriminated himself any further. Shadow sighed. By rights he should probably arrest them both for being accessories and withholding information, but he couldn't see what good it would do. He turned to George.

"What's happening with Bjorn?" he asked.

"We've charged him with burglary and criminal damage so far. He's going to be held on remand at Leeds prison."

At that moment, one of the cell doors swung open and Bjorn appeared in handcuffs with two burly prison officers either side of him. They stood back as he approached the desk to sign the forms George held out for him and turned to Astrid with a sneer.

"Have you come to gloat?" he asked nastily. "Dad might have turned up. If he'd stumped up bail I could be out of here."

"Edward is in hospital," said Dan with a dangerous edge

to his voice.

"Typical! He's a pathetic excuse for a father," replied Bjorn.

Shadow turned to Astrid. "Do you want to tell him or shall I?" he asked.

Astrid stepped forward. "Bjorn, Edward's not your father," she said, bluntly.

"What?" Bjorn looked incredulous.

"I always wondered. Let's face facts – you don't look anything like Edward, so when I bought Dad that DNA test, I also got one for you and me. There's no way you and Edward are related," she said simply without any emotion. "Sadly you and I still are."

"What are you talking about? I never gave any DNA sample," demanded Bjorn. Shadow wondered if the man was capable of ever speaking quietly.

"You snore loudly and sleep with your mouth open," Astrid continued to explain calmly. "I only needed a quick swab."

Bjorn looked outraged. "Can she do that? Is that legal?"

Shadow shrugged. "I've no idea," he replied honestly. "Astrid's the solicitor."

"Anyway, when I found out Mum had been having an affair with Alfred it seemed likely he was your father. Dan took a DNA test and that helped confirm it," continued Astrid evenly. Shadow watched as Bjorn's expression changed from simmering fury to slowly dawning comprehension. He could almost see the pound signs begin to appear in his eyes.

"So, I'm entitled to half Alfred's money," he declared with a grin.

"You're not entitled to anything," Astrid corrected him quickly, her eyes flashing.

Dan placed a calming hand on her shoulder. "You can have one-third," he said, quietly. "Whatever there is, we'll split it equally. A third each for you, me and Will."

"You're giving that idiot a third?" Bjorn began, but before he could say another word Dan had crossed the room and punched him right in the face. Bjorn lay sprawled across the floor with blood pouring from his nose.

"That's enough," ordered Shadow. He pointed to Dan. "Both of you!"

"He wasn't such an idiot when you wanted to pin breaking all those windows on him. You are despicable! When the police have finished with you, I'll agree to you taking a third of whatever Alfred left. Take it or leave it, but you stay away from all of us."

The two prison officers hauled Bjorn to his feet and escorted him out through the back door to the waiting prison van.

"Well, that's one down. Any movement with Plunkett?" he asked George. "Can we expect a London silk to appear for him anytime soon?"

George shook his head and Jimmy looked up from his phone.

"I doubt he'll be able to afford one, Chief. Inspector Hugo says they have asked the banks to freeze his assets while they investigate what else he was getting up to in Guernsey."

"Don't worry, Chief Inspector," Astrid joined in. "There's somebody on the way to assist Mr Plunkett."

Just then there was the sound of heavy footsteps on the stone stairs and Cornelius Rutherford came puffing down. "Afternoon all!" he called out cheerfully. "I thought it was about time someone from the city's legal fraternity should offer Plunkett a helping hand."

"So, you've come to lend a sympathetic ear?" asked Shadow with a cynical smile.

"Yes, well, something like that." The solicitor grinned. "Lead on, George!"

Rutherford followed George down the corridor, where he was let into Plunkett's cell.

"Martin, old boy! Never fear you are not alone," he called out in greeting. Plunkett's response could not be heard.

"Plunkett's not going to be happy, Chief," said Jimmy under his breath.

Shadow grinned. "Beggars can't be choosers, Sergeant."

"I thought I might go, and check Sophie and Will are okay."

"Yes, all right, off you go."

When Jimmy had disappeared, Shadow turned to Astrid.

"Look, I know you have been trying to find out what

happened to your mother. I don't know anything for sure, but I can tell you what I think happened.

"During her work at the coroner's office, Agnetha discovered Plunkett had kept some of the Viking hoard for himself. She confronted him and during that confrontation she either fell or, more likely, was pushed. The reason I suspect foul play is that an ambulance driver reported smelling whisky on her when they arrived, and her alcohol blood count was high.

"Everyone who knew her said she didn't drink and certainly wouldn't when she was pregnant. I suspect Plunkett poured whisky into her mouth so it would seem like she was drunk. I think he also convinced the pathologist at the time to alter the post-mortem results.

"Unfortunately, unless Rutherford can locate and then appeal to Plunkett's conscience, I can't prove any of this. Everyone else involved at the time is either dead or won't talk, I'm afraid."

Astrid had been listening intently to everything he said. When he finished speaking, she silently flung her arms around him and embraced him tightly. Shadow was quite startled and felt himself blush.

"Thank you for trying, Chief Inspector," she said when she finally released him. "It's a relief to know I wasn't imagining all of this, but I won't rest until Plunkett confesses."

Shadow nodded. He understood the young woman's desire to know the truth; he just didn't like her chances.

"I'll do whatever I can to help," he assured her. "Perhaps knowing what happened may help Edward recover too."

"The doctors sounded more positive about him today." Astrid smiled. "They said he might even be able to come home in a week or so."

"I've promised him I won't sell the museum or any part of the collection. We told him about all the treasure Plunkett had kept hold of and how there's a good chance it would be coming to Daneholm too. That seemed to cheer him up," added Dan.

"I'm pleased," said Shadow. "He deserves some good news. You all do."

HALF AN HOUR later, Shadow was back up in the incident room. Everything was now slowly being dismantled.

Plunkett has been charged with several counts of corruption and embezzlement. He would shortly be following Bjorn to Leeds Prison to await trial. Whether they would ever find enough evidence to charge him in connection with Agnetha's death, only time would tell.

Annabel would be spending the night in her cell at the station. Dan had objected strongly to this, but she had insisted she would be fine. When Shadow had left her, she had been drinking tea and chatting to George. Grace, who was frighteningly efficient, had arranged a special hearing before the magistrates first thing in the morning, where she planned to plead her client should be released due to extenuating circumstances. She had already produced a raft of medical reports, Dan would stand any bail, and Shadow had told the Crown Prosecution Service that he had no objections.

Shadow thought how different things might have been had Agnetha lived. Bjorn may have been raised by his natural parents. Would he have turned out differently? Will would never have been born but would Dan and Alfred have had a better relationship? Shadow sighed. The saddest phrase in the English language: "if only". What might his life have been if only Luisa had lived?

There was a noise behind him, and Shadow turned to see Jimmy and Sophie in the doorway.

"Ah, there you both are! Thanks for helping out with Will, Sophie. By the way, I meant to ask you earlier. It seems something dodgy happened with Agnetha's post-mortem. Do you think Donaldson knew anything about it?"

This had been bothering Shadow. Donaldson seemed to know about Alfred and Agnetha, even though their relationship was not common knowledge. Despite his many unpleasant qualities, Shadow had never considered Donaldson to be corrupt. Sophie shook her head.

"He probably heard rumours, Chief. He had just started working as a pathologist back then and there's plenty of gossip about what Prentice got up to even now."

Shadow nodded grimly. Prentice had been the city pathologist at the same time as Grunwell, Shadow's predecessor. The two men were notorious for their corruption. Shadow was about to ask Sophie another question when Jimmy stepped forward.

"Actually, Chief, is it okay if I get off now? We've booked a table at Harker's to celebrate Sophie's birthday," he explained.

"Yes, of course, I hadn't realised," replied Shadow a little embarrassed. He often forgot others had a life away from the station. "Happy birthday, Sophie!"

"Thanks, Chief. Would you like to join us?" Sophie asked.

Shadow smiled. She was being very sweet and kind, but it was obvious the two of them were looking forward to a night alone together, so he shook his head regretfully.

"Thank you, but I have a reservation at Little Sicily."

"No problem. Do you want to see my present from Jimmy?" Without waiting for an answer, Sophie stepped closer and pushed open the neck of her shirt to show a pretty silver necklace and pendant with elaborate scrolled writing. Sophie held it up for him to take a better look, but Shadow could not make out what it said.

"It's my grandma's name in Gaelic," she explained. "Wasn't it lovely of Jimmy to remember what I told him about her?"

"It's very nice, Sophie." Shadow smiled.

"I asked Miss Treanor to design it for me when I called in to see her. And you thought I had no imagination, Chief!" Jimmy laughed.

Shadow watched the two of them leave, then turned to look out of the window. Harker's was a wine bar on St Helen's Square only a few steps from the station. Jimmy was still limping slightly as he crossed the square. Shadow picked up the telephone on the desk and dialled the number he could see etched in gold on to the windows of the wine bar.

"Good evening. I understand you have a table for two booked under the name Chang. Can I arrange to have a bottle of champagne sent to the diners? No, no message, thank you."

Shadow gave his credit card details and replaced the receiver. He smiled to himself. Maybe Jimmy was right – he was getting sentimental.

"Evening, sir, is there anything else you need? Anything I can do to help at all?"

Shadow glanced behind him to see Tom standing in the doorway.

"Yes, Tom, there is, as a matter of fact," replied Shadow, beckoning the young constable over to where he stood by the window.

"Really, sir?" Tom asked eagerly as he came to join him.

"Yes, as you know Sergeant Chang isn't quite one hundred per cent at the moment and there is a very important task he's no longer able to complete."

"I'd be happy to step in, sir."

"Excellent!" Shadow pointed down to the square where Maggie and Harald had just arrived. "Harald needs walking."

Tom's face fell.

"Yes, sir," he replied, his enthusiasm having completely evaporated as he trudged out of the incident room.

Shadow turned back to the window and stared out across St Helen's Square. Below him he watched as Harald dragged Tom away and then Dan, Astrid, and Will appeared. Shadow had never before felt so despondent after solving a case. The thought of how Will would cope without Annabel hung heavily on Shadow. As the three of them walked along, Will paused and pointed to the sky where the falcon could be seen circling overhead. They all watched it swoop and dive above them. Dan and Astrid each threw an arm around Will.

Shadow smiled to himself. They looked like a little family unit. Maybe they would be all right in the end. The three of them continued to watch the sky, as a sudden gust of wind blew a pile of leaves up into the air, which fluttered down and settled on their shadows.

THE END

Want more? Check out John Shadow's adventure in *A Long Shadow*!

Join Tule Publishing's newsletter for more great reads and weekly deals!

A Viking's Shadow Crossword

Across

2. A bat you can't trust hides in this layer (8 letters)

5. Playing a children's game, you must bluff when wearing this (9 letters)

7. The scent at the start of this femme is pure (7 letters)

9. A maternal figure Tom meets her (6 letters)

10. This Norseman may be the Romans' number six monarch (6 letters)

Down

1. It's strange to initially get the low-down on feeling choked (9 letters)

3. A solicitor? At Yale we find many studying (6 letters)

4. His fraudulent behaviour makes him a top cur, really (7 letters)

6. Ulfberht's sharp words are etched here (5 letters)

8. I would hate to fail my relatives (6 letters)

A Viking's Shadow Crossword – Solution

A Viking's Shadow Crossword – Solution

						1. S						
				2. B	E	T	R	A	Y	A	L	
						R						
	3. L					A		4. C				
	A		5. B	L	I	N	D	F	O	L	D	
	W				G			R				
	Y				L			R			6. S
7. P	E	R	F	U	M	E		U			W
	R		A			D		P			O
			M			9. M	O	T	H	E	R
10. V	I	K	I	N	G						D
			L								
			Y								

238

If you enjoyed *A Viking's Shadow,*
you'll love the next book in....

THE CHIEF INSPECTOR SHADOW SERIES

Book 1: *A Long Shadow*

Book 2: *A Viking's Shadow*

Book 3: *Coming October 2021!*

ABOUT THE AUTHOR

H L Marsay always loved detective stories and promised herself that one day, she would write one too. She is lucky enough to live in York, a city full of history and mystery. When not writing, the five men in her life keep her busy – two sons, two dogs and one husband.

Thank you for reading

A VIKING'S SHADOW

If you enjoyed this book, you can find more from all our great authors at TulePublishing.com, or from your favorite online retailer.

TULE
PUBLISHING

34536068R00146